Absence

Absence

Issa Quincy

GRANTA

Granta Publications, 12 Addison Avenue, London W11 4QR
First published in Great Britain by Granta Books, 2025

A CIP catalogue record for this book
is available from the British Library.

1 3 5 7 9 10 8 6 4 2

ISBN 978 1 80351 226 6 (hardback)
ISBN 978 1 80351 227 3 (ebook)

Typeset in Adobe Garamond by Iram Allam
Printed and bound by CPI Group (UK) Ltd, Croydon, CR0 4YY

The manufacturer's authorised representative in the EU for product
safety is Authorised Rep Compliance Ltd, 71 Lower Baggot Street,
Dublin D02 P593, Ireland. www.arccompliance.com

www.granta.com

For F.B.N.

When I think of the time before now, as remote as it seems, it is my mother that I think of. When my thoughts are with her, I think of the poem that I'd so often hear her whispering or reading aloud to herself. As a restless little boy, unable to sleep, she'd sit at the foot of my bed softly singing its passages from a pale-yellow book to lull me to sleep. Even now, so far from those moments, I can still hear the sound of her voice, soft and gentle; distant as to suggest that it, along with her image, is slowly disintegrating in my mind. And so, at times, to suffuse that slowly appearing gap, I read a single line from the poem, or on my laptop I listen to the recording of a stranger reading it aloud. I close my eyes and allow the memories of my mother to surface, and in tunnelling through those narrow passageways, those burnt-out tracts of memory, I find her. I see her again sat there on the edge of my bed, in the half-light, melodically whispering those holy words; words freighted with pain, inflected with years of damage, emanating from the historic and the imperceptible which at such a young and naive age I could not fully grasp but only sense. When I find her there, she is facing away from me, hunched and perched towards the foot of my bed, and I see myself, my limpid and tired eyes watching her dolefully, resisting sleep for fear that, if I were to succumb to it, she would not be there when I woke. Slowly, as her image swells in me, the sound of her reading the poem rings clearer. She talks against the silence like a cry against a storm, and gradually, in this way, my mother re-forms in me, and that inevitable effacement is resisted. I have defeated it for now. It is with her there, so many years past now, I am reminded of who I was before I myself disappeared.

As I became older – as an adolescent – lines from the poem remained cut in small fragments and stuck on her fridge until eventually they fell to the floor, out of sight. When I left my mother's home and moved through the world, encountering and listening to others, for listening is where language both ends and begins, the poem returned to me, perpetually making its way back to me in ways so strange and surprising, I felt cosmically entangled with it, like I would never be able to escape it. At times it felt like the world had its own sly way of reminding me who I was, from when it was I had first walked, even as I dispersed further into nobody at all, into nothing more than a voice without a vessel silently drifting through old images, memories, voices and histories and ever slipping beneath the black water of that ever rising and murky past.

The poem appeared to me again shortly after I turned thirty. I had just returned to my mother's home to help her as her health had deteriorated so severely she'd become unable to complete most day-to-day tasks. It had been during one of those quiet and ambling days that I fell back in touch with an old favourite teacher of mine who had disappeared from our school in the winter of my final year under mysterious and unexplained circumstances. Following his departure, my peers and I would often ask our teachers in class what had happened to him, and each lunchbreak we would scour the news for any information. There was always nothing, nothing other than a resounding and suspicious silence. By the time I had left school we all presumed that he was dead, and by the time he first reappeared to me I had spent so long not knowing that when I finally came to understand the reason that he had suddenly left our school all those years before, I wasn't quite sure how to feel or how to react.

I first saw Mr Rothlan again more than a decade since I'd last done so at school. It was one of those empty days that slouches freely into the next. I had been walking up to a now-closed grocer on Magdalen Road to collect a list of ingredients, hastily scribbled by my ailing mother, when I spotted him on the opposite side of the road with an exhausted and rugged look etched into his face. He walked with the same odd gait he always had: balling his weight onto his heels and springing up onto his toes with his arms straight down and unmoving beside his hips. Doubtless, he had seen me and subsequently made an awkward and somewhat embarrassing attempt to avoid my gaze: unconvincingly looking up and away at the sullen red-brick Samaritans building to his left. But I'd already seen him and called out eagerly, *Mr Rothlan!*

I recall him feigning surprise at seeing me so poorly (like a street mime artist) that I struggled to suppress my smile as he crossed unsteadily over to my side of the road. He was unnaturally unkempt: wearing stained jogging bottoms too short and a baggy white T-shirt that in parts clung to the dampness of his skin. Slung across his shoulder he held a navy swimming bag from which a bundled towel flopped partially out. We spoke for some time there and he explained how each day he swam in the local council pool. He expressed to me his enjoyment of that pool – despite it famously being the smallest and dirtiest – over the others in the city simply because, as he put it to me, *It is emptier than the rest.* Only when thinking of that encounter years later did I trace beneath his words his want for privacy spring forth as a kind of veiled admission, one which at the time I didn't understand the reason for. He seemed to be withholding something. As much was clear in his attempt to ignore me, in his distracted gaze that moved between my eyes and the pavement and further off down the road. It was uncharacteristic of him, but then again I was seeing a different man to the once brilliant teacher I'd known. I was presented instead with a feeble and impotent figure who had been bowed and broken by something he wasn't willing to reveal to me.

We spoke for only a few moments. I told him of some of the authors I'd been reading, names which he smiled at, knowing these were all ones he'd suggested to me in class. Seeing him so undone, I was overcome by a burrowing sadness which moved from me a sudden burst of anxious concern for him: I explained that I appreciated his classes and his teaching and had been *Sad to see him leave* – remarks

I immediately regretted making when I noticed him fall into the wordless stupor that tends to be provoked by the rising of the past above one's mouth. His gaze fell down to his scuffed black leather shoes, his lips slightly trembled and his right hand, very steadily, rubbed the whiskers of white hair on his head. Several times in that short moment did he seem to attempt speech, and each time he stopped his words. Words I will never know. Returning gradually to the present, he suggested I join him and his dear friend Gilles, a scholar at the university on Hume (who I already knew distantly through family), for dinner at his house on Cherwell Street.

I had always felt as though Mr Rothlan and I had a unique student–teacher relationship. We frequently talked after class, discussions which often left me late for my next class, or if lunch or dinner followed the lesson, we'd walk together from the classroom to the dining hall and along the way we'd discuss the books and essays he'd told me to read or the films he'd impressed the cruciality upon me to watch. This led me to believe that he had a special interest in my abilities despite me being an otherwise disinterested student. He inspired something in me, pried it out of me, and his invitation to me then, all those years later, felt like the offer of an extension to our relationship.

I recall being oddly taken aback at seeing his house, it was a modest terraced one-up, one-down with two windows, both parallel to the door, and a bare patch of brick directly above it that betrayed basic symmetry, which bothered me. The flooring was stripped hardwood planks, misshapen and distorted over time, that shifted beneath you as you walked and between which blew a stone-chill draught. His living room was composed of a floor-to-ceiling, wall-to-wall bookshelf, a dusty couch and two torn armchairs that were in dire need of re-upholstering. In the centre of the room stood a flimsy, cheap-seeming coffee table with a neat stack of periodicals and some tea-stained coasters. The kitchen was thin and ill-designed and extended backwards into a small concrete garden without pots or plants, only a metal garden chair and a forgotten pale-blue mug half-full of rain-water. There were no familial or personal photos anywhere. Instead images of Cocteau's drawings I recognized from *Les Enfants Terribles* covered the walls of his hallway, a large sepia portrait of Pasolini's gaunt and sculpted face watched over the living room, while in the bathroom there was a framed black-and-white photograph of Edith Piaf, holding herself as she sang, looking up into a spotlight as though looking out onto the world, alone yet unafraid of it, beside a much smaller picture of Thierry Henry celebrating a goal.

For dinner, sat beneath a low-hanging bulb, we ate a poorly cooked but well-intended pasta dish and briefly discussed our favourite season, the sweetest hymns, the best brand of tea available in supermarkets, and the assassination of Patrice Lumumba and the Aimé Césaire play that followed it. Mostly, however, Gilles talked about his poor health: he had suffered from tuberculosis as a boy and undergone surgery for it that resulted in, at times, debilitating respiratory issues that had plagued him since and caused him to talk with a gravelly wheeze, which pronounced itself at the end of each sentence. Mr Rothlan jokingly made a point (which had clearly been made continuously throughout their friendship) to stress the unsettling similarity that his life bore to the famous French philosopher with whom he also shared a first name. To this, Gilles angrily proclaimed, *My God, Iain! He was just fifteen when I was born; it is only chance we share so many biographical similarities,* as well as saying with a degree of smug cynicism that was characteristic of him. *Besides, I have absolutely no intention to end my life the way that he did his,* and Mr Rothlan, I recall, replied to this in a way that has remained with me since: *But that choice is the most human of all choices.*

This would be the first of several times that I would visit Mr Rothlan before his death.

My former teacher was found after Gilles grew worried when he had failed to answer his door a number of times and missed two engagements he had previously agreed to attend. Containing his worry for long enough, one wintry night, Gilles accompanied two police officers to Mr Rothlan's door and despite the officers ordering Gilles to *Wait outside, don't come in,* he waited only a few seconds (fourteen exactly) before following them in through the low and austere hallway, the same hallway that Gilles had walked through so many times before, when greeting or parting, meeting or waiting for his dear old friend. Only this time, Gilles noticed a difference in the house: in the corners of the walls, which usually collected darkness, there was instead a diaphanous

7

quality to them like translucent bundles of light were caught jittering there, static and humming. Sensing this and taking it as no illusion of the mind but what instead he called 'true knowing', Gilles rushed right up to the bedroom and was met by the sight of his dear old friend's body hanging in that odd way that bodies hang – both entirely limp and completely rigid and shamefully facing away from the eyes of his only friend and those of the two strangers.

When Gilles first recalled that night to me, he explained how when the officers entered the house and disappeared from his sight, he knew that Mr Rothlan was dead: *When I couldn't see them anymore, it was as though the officers slipped momentarily into his state, or non-state rather. And as I watched them vanish into his house, I knew he was gone too.* When in response I asked Gilles what he meant by this; how could he possibly know from the simple fact of the officers entering a dark house that his friend was dead, he couldn't quite answer me. He floundered and grasped for something to say, some words to make plain his feeling, but when, after trying and failing, he fell silent, exasperated and annoyed at himself for being so inarticulate. I knew not to press any further. Besides, in a sense, I understood what he meant: in that particular moment, he had felt the tremor of a true and deep-rooted spirit, an impulsive intuition that was – owing to the length of his and Mr Rothlan's shared history – impossible to explain to anyone outside of that particular passage of time. It is that which can only be felt, maybe even visualized but never verbalized.

(I recall once reading in the news about a mother whose child had gone missing. After a day or two of extensive regional searches for the child, at a press conference, the mother, after remaining silent beside her stern and pleading husband, proclaimed wildly and suddenly that her child was dead. After a brief and confused pause she was questioned about her statement and she explained to the reporters – rather eloquently, I thought – that she had woken up crying that morning after a string of nightmarish dreams and an overbearing feeling, one she hadn't ever felt before, of her child no longer being on earth. Of course, the mother's words were disregarded as simply originating of a kind of hallucinatory grief, but some days later her child was found dead. The coroner ruled that the child had died some days earlier, to be exact: on the day the mother had woken up crying.)

By the time the fact of his passing had reached me, Mr Rothlan had been dead for little over a week and a strange silence lingered around it: it wasn't in the news nor was there any kind of *In Memoriam* email from my former school (the school he had taught at for over a decade), there wasn't any chatter between those that knew him and nor did there seem to be any family of Mr Rothlan's to mourn him or organize his belongings. It was instead left up to Gilles to clear out his home, rifle through his old friend's things and to enact his will, which decreed that his possessions be donated (he named five charities) or recycled (near his home).

It was Gilles who revealed Mr Rothlan's passing to me while also asking of me a strange favour, *To pass on a letter to a*

9

former peer of yours, from Iain. The front of the letter bore the name of the boy and was written in my former teacher's usual scrawled and looping hand. The peer of mine was known to me despite being in the year below, and his name was one that I hadn't heard since I'd left school. Recalling to myself the times the boy had been mentioned, I found they were all often in passing, to mock him or when a female friend of mine would point out how uncomfortable she felt around him like he were some freak. He was a timid boy who rarely spoke and one who seemed entirely contained within himself and content in passing through school (and life?) unnoticed, in fact, happier that way.

The boy reluctantly agreed to meet me so that I could give him the letter. We chose to meet in Florence Park, a public park close to my mother's home and not far from his own.

It was a sharp, mid-winter morning. The park was entirely empty and the trees dripped a black dew. The air was filled with a thinning mist that I remember obscured the park I had played in many times as a child in an achromatic grey. As I worked my way through the intersecting concrete footpaths with my visibility diminished, I felt unsure of my footing. Even despite my acquaintance with the park's banks and paths, the trees and its avenues, the grounds felt faintly indeterminate like I were passing through a distant but dear memory, battling the effects of both familiarity and foreignness.

I found the boy sat on a bench staring at a row of bare flower beds: the empty mud was topped with a dainty layer of frost that gave the earth a fragile and beautiful veneer. The boy, who was now in fact a young man, was sat shivering with his coat wrapped tightly around him. He'd hung his scarf through itself and had his hands nestled deeply into his pockets. Because of the rigid cold and the cold alone, instead of shaking hands we faintly tilted our heads at each other, hoping to signify some vague acknowledgement between us. Before I sat, he asked if we could walk, *Just to warm up*, so we moved towards the north of the park, at first walking in total and tired silence.

I wasn't sure whether to offer him the letter immediately and be done with it or to converse with him. I hadn't read the letter's contents and was desperate to understand why my former Languages teacher, Mr Rothlan, an eccentric and brilliant individual, an unorthodox teacher and maverick mind, was in any way connected to this fairly innocuous and unremarkable student so much as to write him a letter that required delivery by hand. Despite my doubts and considerations, in the end it didn't require my talking, as the young man began by asking me questions about Mr Rothlan's death and so, I explained to him, brashly and without much affect, that the old man had committed suicide by hanging in his bedroom closet and was found by Gilles, his old and only friend.

The news seemed to further quieten the young man, as if a remote part of him contracted a little more, and now his disposition, both verbal and physical, was burdened with ever-increasing pressure and his speech from then on was confused but delicate like the sound of glass shards hitting the ground: tinkling, felt, all at once.

He asked me about the letter and I explained that I hadn't any idea of its contents, that I hadn't so much as looked at it and lied to him in saying that I hadn't the slightest interest in what it said either. Yet in spite of making my disinterest clear, as we passed under the sodden bough of an oak tree, heading towards the empty tennis courts, he stopped and turned to me, catching my gaze for the first time, and as voices so seek to sculpt themselves, to give distinction to the tangled meshing of their hidden images, he slowly and rather painstakingly explained to me the nature of his and Mr Rothlan's relationship.

Before I continue, I ought to recall the final time that I saw Mr Rothlan. He invited me over to his home for tea, and in the dimness of his living room we sat and spoke well into the evening. While the conversation we had felt to occupy at least some great importance in my mind (perhaps solely due to my unwavering admiration for the man) I have forgotten nearly all of it. That is other than the few words he began with and some final words about his family and his upbringing. This is what I can recall:

Outside Warrington, 1952

In a town that sits equidistant between Manchester and Liverpool, Iain Gregory Rothlan was born to Iain Rothlan

Sr, a worker at a local chemical plant and Mary-Lou Larkin, a mother of five, both devout Catholics. His family were of Irish descent, his father arriving as a young boy in Liverpool in the early 1930s on the SS *Lady Munster*.

Mr Rothlan explained that each Christmas Iain Rothlan Sr would insist upon visiting his remaining family in Cork, and with each passing year, and with the number of family members dwindling, Mr Rothlan's father would compel his children and Mary-Lou to join him in taking the slow ferry back to Ireland that set from Liverpool.

I believe, Mr Rothlan confessed of his father, *that his insistence on making this trip came from him wanting us to experience the same distress he had suffered at the hand of his father when he suddenly forced his family to England in search of work. This led them away from their friends and the rest of their family and was deeply painful for them all. An incredible cruelty. Or, perhaps*, he said softly, *it was as a means of reliving it himself. I mean, making that traumatic passage, like it was an act of masochism that arose from his feeling guilt at abandoning his brawny rural roots. But perhaps*, he tried again somewhat more exhaustedly, *even that is rather far-fetched and it is simply without him knowing, when he left Ireland, he had begun a ritual that he'd go on to complete almost every year for the remainder of his life, as so many of us do.* When he said this to me, I recall Mr Rothlan pressed the side of his thick index finger to his lips, nodded and eventually, after many minutes, moralized: *I suppose, we are all constantly in the process of ritual-making, falling deeply into ones and forgetting others.*

We don't stop ritualizing until we forget it, and after that it is forgetting that becomes ritual.

Mr Rothlan then described to me one such Christmas boat-journey, one he described as being *Impressed upon my memory like the mark of a crumbling flower upon a page of a diary.* He was just sixteen and was embarking on what would become his penultimate return to Ireland: *It had been one of those miserable and gloomy December mornings you grow accustomed to in this part of the world, where the sea reflected grey skies, cancelling all and any colours aboard the boat or beyond. As we always did, my father and I spent some minutes – despite the spray of cold rain and cutting wind – on the front deck of the boat watching as Ireland, beneath the broken clouds, at last came into view. When we approached land, my father pointed out Lambay Island as it emerged through the mist, the sea stacks surrounding Ireland's Eye, the striped chimneys of Dublin port and at last, Sugarloaf and the Wicklow Mountains, which appeared out of the grey fog that receded from the shoreline, sort of cupping the city within them. At the time, we had been sharing the deck with fellow passengers, most of them young children wanting to watch the bow cut the thrashing sea and hoping to spot a seal or whale in the water.*

As Iain Rothlan Sr pointed out and talked about a Martello tower with the same story and same words he used every year about the same tower, Mr Rothlan noticed a young boy no older than ten leaning over the edge of the boat as it crested a wave, eager to see the sea foam thrusted apart by the liner or perhaps, as Mr Rothlan opined to me with anguish, the boy spotted a seal and sought, as children often do, to follow it from over the rail for as long as the seal permitted. But as the boat bounced up over a wave, the boy swung over the edge and was suddenly swallowed by the unctuous water.

He resurfaced rather quickly, Mr Rothlan recalled mournfully, *and flailed on the surface. His face was contorted and helpless, his eyes stricken with fear. I can't escape the sight of the boy's mother and the sorrow with which she cried his name over and over again, no other words, no cries to God, only his name and never for help like she knew his fate. There were no ring buoys on the deck and she tried to jump over the edge but was stopped by a crowd of people. When someone did eventually arrive with a buoy, the ship had long passed and the boy had since sunk into the sea whose waves fell totally still. Across the deck a silence descended. People raced to console the family but my father, when all had settled, waited a moment before continuing with his story of the Martello tower, like death was no distant stranger and where at once it had extinguished dreams and memories right before us, it too was a part of that inevitable metamorphosis: that forever things changed and on they'd continue, no differently to the manner in which the boat pulled into Dublin harbour and we all disembarked. As with all things, the tragedy of the boy was slowly shuffled to the back of our focus and most of us soon forgot. But I couldn't, no matter how I tried. I couldn't ever seem to forget and now I see it was less to do with the boy and more to do with the indifference of my father.*

Mr Rothlan recalled to me the anger and resentment he felt towards his father for this, and from that moment Mr

Rothlan began an act of distancing himself from him that would in fact last his entire life, growing with each passing day. He was never able to shake the face of the boy's mother or cry of the boy's name, and the boy would visit him in dreams and visions so vivid that the sense realized in Mr Rothlan was one of guilt that he hadn't done more. He explained to me that he felt as though he were somehow at fault for the boy's death despite knowing he had no part in it nor any way of assisting in the tragedy. The apathy, however, of Iain Rothlan Sr was doubtless what birthed this guilt in Mr Rothlan. He felt shame in his father's inhumanity that turned to disgust, and which inevitably resulted in Mr Rothlan not facing his father again until the old man lay supine in a coffin at the age of fifty-two after suffering a short spell of asbestosis.

After that particular trip to Ireland, Mr Rothlan explained to me, *I was granted early admission to Cambridge where I studied Modern and Medieval Languages, and after my graduation I took up a number of different posts in the Middle East and North Africa: in Beirut, Libya and finally Syria. I worked mostly in risk consultancy but in translation too, and in my early thirties I returned to England and gained admission to Oxford to study International Affairs for my Masters. After finishing at Oxford, a city which to my mind is far superior to Cambridge, I was offered a job in policymaking in the United States.* A job that he would explain he declined and decided instead, after meeting a man he would describe to me as his *first and only love in this world*, to remain in Oxford and take up teaching. He began as a lecturer at Oxford Brookes University, or Oxford Polytechnic as it was known then, but quickly became disenchanted with academia and decided to take a role at a local state school. He did this happily for seven years and rather successfully too; he eventually succumbed to the offer of becoming the Academic Director of an independent school, a position which he quit within two weeks, while remaining as a Languages teacher at the same school for close to twelve years before, of course, abruptly leaving in the middle of my final year.

The young man stopped in front of a laurel bush and inspected my face closely. He was taller than I remembered, there were the scars of pimples pitted across his cheeks, and a burgeoning rail of stubble along his chin. He had long, thin eyebrows that nearly connected in the middle and his hair, choppy and brown, was greasy and hastily shoved to the left. He had a kind face and dark eyes, around the edges of which I noticed an exhaustion that he had so far attempted to resist.

He explained to me that he and Mr Rothlan had been engaged in a sexual relationship for two years, from when he was fifteen years old until he was seventeen. *I was in awe of him. I was a bad student. I skipped classes and he brought something out of me, a desire to care, to learn. I fell in love with the books he gave me to read, but more than that I loved the movies he told me to watch, you know, Truffaut and Bresson, Marker and Varda, and soon I found myself wanting to direct my own films and to make them in the style of those directors. The way he spoke to me about them having their own language, the ones they'd created, made me feel as though I could also create my*

own language with images and sounds, my own system through
which to understand and misunderstand the world.

Upon hearing this, I lapsed into that same speechlessness, inner soundlessness, that I had when I heard of the old man's death. A Gordian knot of disgust, pain but, above all, uncertainty fluttered through me so quickly I became hollow, unsure what to say, what to feel, and this sense remained trapped within me in the weeks, months and a few years after I was first told. Only now, some years since, have I come to notice more sharply, more distinctly, against all other opinion, in that strange and precarious place within me, a lambent sense of tragedy for my former teacher.

The young man went on: painstakingly detailing to me the advice that Mr Rothlan had imparted upon him, the example he led by, and the sensitivity with which he thought and critiqued himself and the vicious world that he found himself trapped within. He recalled to me, in what became an almost soundless mutter of monotony, various intimate resonances and anecdotes: the evenings they'd spend in the Languages building watching films from a projector, and afterwards how they'd sit and talk in the darkened classrooms before walking home together as they lived close to one another.

As the young man spoke, recalling the various intimate details, I felt the quietening of an illusion in me. I realized then that my own relationship with Mr Rothlan, albeit platonic, hardly grazed the surface of what this boy and Mr Rothlan had shared. I became enraged, bitter, jealous even of him, and then realizing I hadn't yet handed him the letter, I thought to hold onto it and read it; I thought to tear it up, to never hand it over, and as these feelings washed over me, almost reflexively, rather suddenly, as he was mid-sentence, I passed him the letter.

In the boy's penultimate year, his parents found a tranche of text messages, notes and emails between Mr Rothlan and their son and immediately informed the school, who immediately informed the police, who immediately arrested Mr Rothlan and charged him.

The mist was gone by then. We crossed a bridge that rose above a brook slowly lapping over grey stones and fallen brown sticks. As we walked, the young man told me of the shame that he was made to feel by his parents. *It was hell. My father wouldn't even look at me most days and my mother was left to interact with me alone, which for months she struggled with. Months passed by. I couldn't leave my bed and would remain for the longest hours of the day in a dark and dirty room, avoiding any contact and conflict with the world beyond the one I'd created for myself. I fell behind on my studies, and on some days I would struggle to remain in classes, often rushing out in fits of panic to the health centre. On other days, I was unable to even make it into school, and eventually, after a series of meetings between myself, my parents and my teachers, my teachers and my parents, my teachers and I, I was asked to leave. It was almost two years later that I eventually came to realize I couldn't go on as I was. I had put on weight and had become so unhealthy that people I'd known for years no longer recognized me. Where was the life after this? There wasn't one.*

When I questioned him as to what he meant by this, he explained that the life he lived was not life but instead the life of a dead person. He saw no one, not even the light outside of his room. He filled his time with protracted and painful silences; he despised the world that he made up, coming to hate both his parents and yet relying solely and increasingly upon them. When his friends, concerned and anxious, would visit the house to check on him he would tell them to *Fuck off.* He would abuse his mother and feared his father, and would wait for him to depart from the house before leaving his own room. He'd hear his father muttering insults whenever they crossed paths, or shouting from through the floorboards, *I want him out of my fucking house.* Soon thereafter, he left home but not before endlessly tunnelling through the narrow and dark channels of thought that always seemed to land upon that final question: *And if I weren't here?*

Within months, he signed on for benefit payments, took some money from his mother and eventually was allocated a council flat above an elderly couple in a low-rise housing complex in Littlemore. He began working at a cinema in an expansive and empty entertainment complex on the edge of the city, spending his shifts shovelling popcorn and pouring large fizzy drinks for teenagers who had bunked off school. And in the evenings and mornings, he would speak to his neighbours and discuss small things: *When the roofing will be done; If I've spoken to the management about the leak under the kitchen sink; If I want to go round for dinner with them,* which he always did.

Even despite this marked change in him, although on the surface there seemed to be something positive that echoed through him as he described these things with a forceful pride, the young man felt a great aloneness within him, and after spending most of his nights absorbing the old images and sounds of films he'd once aspired to make he'd lie wondering what lay ahead for him, sleeping beneath a black mould that would eventually be left for so long it would cause him to be hospitalized; he'd think about the joy he once felt in his life and wondered if he'd ever feel it again, and with each day providing further distance from that feeling he'd come to wonder if he'd ever felt it at all, if he ever had the capacity to feel like he once did; a feeling he had to imagine now, a feeling he couldn't be certain of and, naturally, he'd think about what he had lost, what he no longer had in the moment of his thinking that he had had in his moment of feeling, and he'd mourn those things with a naked grief that usually arose in the hours of the night when he was most alone and drifting with ease between the world of dream and the inconstancy of actuality; between here and somewhere beyond reach; between the misery of the present and the dilation of the past which bloated into a shadowy distance. There was something behind him and nothing lay ahead of him, and in these moments he'd think of his teacher, Mr Rothlan, the one who had given him something to grab hold of, the one who whistled at the embers in him, the one who despite what he'd been told – how *Sick, Wrong, Repulsive, Disgusting* the old man was – he still missed and thought of every day and would continue thinking of every day, every minute, every fraction of a second right up to when he walked to the edge of the multi-storey car park near his home to throw himself from just two years after I met with him in the park.

I remember we walked on to a bench and talked a little more but quickly our conversation dissipated into an uninterested silence. I thought about the letter and what it might mean for him to read Mr Rothlan's words; I wondered what the words were. I imagined that the letter might change his disposition, his confidence and his energy. I wondered if it might enliven something in him or that it might provide some degree of closure that would be important for him to have, important for him to relight the dim glow that still burned in him, somewhere. But this was my blind faith in words, nothing more. The more I reckoned with what might occur if he opened it, the more I could see the stark reality burgeoning through my visions of him. He might not read the letter at all. He might, in fact, throw it away as soon we parted, discard it in some bin along a path or simply drop it into the brook unopened. The words might forever remain unknown.

He eventually said he had to go and stood to shake my hand. As I rose to meet him, he reminded me of his name again and I realized then it was the same name as the boy that Mr Rothlan had watched drown as a teenager, the same name the boy's mother had called, *Over and over . . .*

After realizing this, I wanted to speak to Gilles about it. He asked me to meet him in Mr Rothlan's house on Cherwell Street as he was in the process of sorting out most of the clutter. The house was half-cleared and the trembling air that Gilles had told me about in those first weeks immediately after Mr Rothlan's death had seemed to still. No longer did it tremble or pulse with anything other than its own quiet darkness, and I shivered at the whip of a numbing cold air that blew through from the garden, into the thin kitchen and the hall. Hunched in a corner beside the sofa, Gilles was rifling through a number of books. He had taken a slim edition of one in his hand and turned it over in his palm, inspecting the cover, muttering to himself as he did.

From the doorway, I couldn't make out what the book was, but it was an old edition; the pages were yellowed and crumbled as he thumbed through them. I crouched on the other side of the room to help him, and as we packed away some books into boxes in the living room I posed the coincidence to him of the names of the two boys in the vague hope he might offer some mystic answer to it, some psychological resolution that would provide a kind of causal root to confirm my belief that it was, in fact, not a coincidence. But he ignored my query, still holding the book, reading through it and tracing the lines with a finger, muttering them into the walls of the silent house. Eventually, he looked up at me, as though breaking from a kind of trance, he said with a sunken smile, *Iain loved this one dearly. He used to read to me from it and recite the passages after dinners.* I asked Gilles if he heard my question, but again he had slipped into that sacred silence, following the lines with his finger quicker and quicker now, seemingly hoping to find a specific passage in the text. I continued to pack away some books into two separate boxes as Gilles had stopped entirely. Until at last, he perked up and intoned in a low voice like a minister reading his orisons:

> *He is at peace – this wretched man –*
> *At peace, or will be soon:*
> *There is no thing to make him mad,*
> *Nor does Terror walk at noon,*
> *For the lampless Earth in which he lies*
> *Has neither Sun nor Moon.*

He thumbed forward a page and then began reading again:

> *Yet all is well; he has but passed*
> *To Life's appointed bourne:*
> *And alien tears will fill for him*
> *Pity's long-broken urn,*
> *For his mourners will be outcast men,*
> *And outcasts always mourn.*

I knew almost immediately the text that he was reading from but didn't respond as though I did. A strange kind of fatigue had numbed me, and the effort, the usual determination with which I would want to explain my connection to the poem, sank beneath a heavy cloud of sudden and unremitting exhaustion. Gilles lay the book onto his great-coat which was folded over the arm of the sofa and together we continued to sort through the books, separating them into different boxes, some for donation and others for recycling. As I continued with the task, my thoughts of the young boy, of Mr Rothlan, dissolved beneath a grey that refused to recede and my mind became blank, totally empty, just as when I was a boy lying in bed as my mother read to me from the poem she loved so much and I listened to her, thoughtless, mute, allowing images to form in me only for them to quickly wash away again.

In the Rijksmuseum in Amsterdam, there is a painting by Hendrick Avercamp, the mute of Kampen, hung on a deadening grey felt and squeezed in amid other Dutch masters. One's initial glance at the painting will see it reveal little more than a benign winter scene. However, when you look at Avercamp's painting closely you begin to notice the close detailing of the variance of life. There in the painting exists death, pleasure, ecstasy, frivolity, poverty and secrecy, closely exacted alongside other states of being and non-being all perceived by Avercamp from a heightened position, a vantage point for an incorporeal observer; a drifting onlooker that watches and takes in the immediate while the rest of the yellow-grey land and sky disperse outwards into misty incomprehensibility. What is presented is the sight of the intangible spectator that sees what is in front of him, recognizes everything and curtails his judgement of anything.

In Eastern Massachusetts, there are three identical buildings that protrude out of the soft brown earth. They are dense redbrick high rises. Each one perfectly equidistant from the other. Along the face of each building is an endless number of windows that on certain days, in certain lights, with the sun shimmering off them, seem to ripple like great red undulations flashing as you drive in their shadow.

This was not how I first saw them.

When I was seven years old, my parents made a doomed and brief move to Boston; for work for my father, to be nearer to her family for my mother. This move would only last three years, and resulted in my parents return to England, and their divorce that same year. In that time, however, when my mother and father were busy, I'd often be left in the company of my grandmother, whom I frequently accompanied by car around town. When going to either the cinema or the grocery store we'd drive to Fresh Pond Mall. To get there, we wound down tree-lined streets, verdant suburbs and on past old and newly painted colonial houses with damp wooden facades and Boston-blue trimmed windows to eventually arrive at the shopping centre from behind, not from off the Alewife Brook Parkway, not from past Fresh Pond itself – an old pond from which Native Americans would fish for alewives and drink from, a pond which you can skate on in the winter.

When you arrive at Fresh Pond via the back entrance you must drive across an overgrown portion of abandoned railway line that was once a part of the Watertown Branch Railroad. In the autumn, you can follow this trail round through Cambridge, and with the shimmering leaves scattered around you, you feel warmed by their fervent colours even against the bite of the sharp Atlantic air, like you're ensconced within the roar of an ancient funeral pyre.

It was snowing when I first saw the towers. I remember the day as being emptied of life. Thick snowdrifts were piled high on the roadsides and an ice-thin wind whipped around me. I remember scowling as a young boy at the sight of the towers, believing them to be miserable and seemingly abandoned, despite knowing little about them. When I think back to it, or rather when the images resurface in me thoughtlessly, the disturbance I felt at seeing the towers I now know related less to the immediate structural nature of them and more to the looming symbolism of refuge, endless corridors and hidden lives consigned to the silently suffocating margins of this world. The feelings of imposition and silence, more cognate than we think, are ones that have haunted me since and continue to, even now. I believe that this nauseate moment as a young boy was the source of these sparring powers that have beleaguered my thinking since.

The fact that the buildings could elicit such an immature revulsion and wonder in me as a young boy spoke to the imposing power of these looming structures. Often, from the backseat of her car, I would ask my grandmother why they had even been built in the first place. *For people to live in,* she'd respond, but this answer, which she would repeat to me each time I asked seemed both detached and uncaring and in some way to be lazy; an obvious answer that didn't reveal to me what I hoped it would despite the fact, of course, she was right. As a boy, I could never make sense of the towers, like their very presence sat contrary to the land that they occurred of. It seemed they had erupted through deep fissures in the ground, steaming up from the hissing depths of a terrain entirely unlike the one they now domineered.

After finishing school, little more than a decade after my boyish judgement of them, I moved to Boston to work for a year, and the three towers came back into my view. At the time, I was working as a kitchen porter in a narrow restaurant called Les Sablons in Harvard Square. The restaurant, an old MBTA bus terminal, had been repurposed into a French eatery. Buses still ran past it, stopping and starting beside it, and there drivers changed shifts, some pausing for a smoke and a conversation as if the altered interior of the building hadn't at all changed the operation that had for so long run within it.

February 2004

It was quiet at the restaurant. I had taken a smoke break and come out from the heat of the kitchen into the snowy evening when I asked a woman sat in a faded blue bus driver's uniform on a bench for a lighter. *You're British? What the hell you over here for?* she cackled as smoke seeped through the gaps in her teeth, revealing one or two gold crowns.

She was a weathered woman: her life written into her skin in the etchings of her smiles and the lines of her frowns. She wore her hair in carefully maintained coiling curls that bounced just above her shoulders and a gold Cuban link chain with a Jesus-piece pendant turned the wrong way on her chest, his callow and mournful expression shying away from me, nestled into her bosom. Beneath photochromic glasses, her eyes studied me vaguely. *Patricia, or Pat,* was her name. She was a bus driver for the MBTA. *I was born in Harlem*, she explained, *and grew up way up there on 151st street, the Harlem River houses. I came here to Boston about thirty years ago now. With my son.* When I asked her why she left, without hesitation and in a stony and resolute voice she said, *I didn't have a choice. It was dangerous for me. It was dangerous for my son. I couldn't tell no one there. I just had to go. And one night, he was out, I don't know, working or drinking, something like that. I took my son and we upped and left, got on the coach. We didn't look back. No one knew. We just had to go.* She then paused and softly said again, *There wasn't a choice. It was . . . What they call it?* a wry grin suddenly curling across her face, *A matter of safety,* she said mimicking my British accent before chuckling to herself.

I clearly remember that even with her incessant smoking (a pack of Marlboro Lights a day), which had grazed her voice down to a hoarse drone, she managed to maintain the fragrance of a sweet and sharp perfume that I subsequently discovered to be '1000' by Jean Patou. Patricia would later tell me that they had discontinued it, and that when she found this out she went online and bulk-bought as much as she could. And even then, over a decade after it had stopped being manufactured, she'd find herself trawling eBay and outmoded webstores for any lingering bottles.

When I first smelt it on her an odd sense overcame me. It was the scent of paling summer evenings spent at dinner tables as a bored young boy listening to the drone of adult conversation circling around. Where distant and alien-sounding regions like *Helmand* and *Basrah* and words like *fiscal* and *unjustifiable* were frequently uttered and re-uttered with increasing fury long into the night. And as well, upon smelling her perfume, I found myself lost in a memory (that I can't be sure was not a fabrication) of being sat at my grandmother's house as a boy, leaning wearily into a garden chair, my gaze fixed on the tree swing wobbling in the wind as uncles and family friends fumbled over a grill. A breeze would blow and I'd become cold and slap the mosquitoes on my arms and legs as I lay there happily watching as the gathering evening that had lengthened around us became punctured by the starry glints of fireflies.

Those thoughts, however, were washed away by the sudden blue-black darkness outside the restaurant, as well as the conversation that had ensued between Patricia and me as we shivered in the soft and vanishing snow. I told Patricia that I had finished school and was working here before I hopefully would be able to continue my studies somewhere. *But tell me about England*, she said with a smile, *I wanna know about London and where you grew up. I've always wanted to go there. Believe me, I will soon. And what about this restaurant, any good? I heard it's expensive.* I gave her the answers that I gave everyone: mechanical ones that I had perfected in the time I'd spent there like they were the lines of a script.

Despite all the distractions of the evening and the transience of our encounter, I didn't forget the first sense I had when I met her and smelt the perfume she wore. I had been overcome with indiscernible feelings, scattered memories and images that I couldn't piece together. It is true, to some extent, that her smell nudged at something in me that I wasn't yet sure of and called down to some forgotten part of me. *It's my only luxury*, she would later repeat defensively to me whenever the struggle of living costs arose in conversation, *It's my treat to myself.*

Years before, Patricia had come into contact with the perfume through an old lady who would take the bus from Harvard Square to Fresh Pond to feed the ducks each morning. After almost a year of her boarding the bus and the two of them talking, Patricia asked the elderly woman which perfume she wore as she liked the scent. The old lady refused to tell her, saying with a wink, *Not until I am closer to death.* And when one morning, five years after first getting on, Patricia helped the old lady – who was by this point immeasurably frail and required a carer to attend to her – off the bus, the old lady whispered, *Patou '1000'*. Patricia knew naturally that would be the last time she would see the old lady and it was. For Patricia, wearing the perfume felt like *A kind of inheritance.*

In the time I worked at Les Sablons I came to know Patricia more as our shifts and breaks began to align; much like when there comes a certain natural, biological alignment in the early stages of a symbiotic relationship, one that seems entirely organic but is in fact willed into being from both sides, either unconsciously or consciously.

You remind me of my son, Patricia told me one afternoon, *You aren't like him . . . But you remind me of him . . . It's something in you. I don't know what.* Patricia told me she wasn't in touch with her son. She never told me anything more. His name. His age. Anything. She only had had one boy. She never told me what had happened between the two of them and I never asked, as to me there remain certain things, many things, that do not require words to be understood: the change in her gaze, the contortion of her posture, the manner in which her smile would fade and silence seeped into her person whenever her thoughts distracted her and they were only of her son. All this quietened my own curiosity like the silence I kept granted her the space she didn't allow herself.

Often Patricia and I would talk about the news. She would lament the escalation of prescription opioid usage that she saw quietly, even then, as a problem in her community in Boston, and with each passing ambulance she would say, *There goes another off them fucking pills*, with a kind of matter-of-factness and disdain.

I remember arriving at South Station late one night off a Greyhound bus. It was around 3 a.m. and I wanted to buy a pack of cigarettes. Because of the recently changed laws, I was no longer able to legally do so, and so instead I cantered around the station looking for someone old enough to buy them for me. Outside, beside two backpacks resting against the wall, I spotted two young men leaning on one of the exits at the corner of Atlantic Avenue and Summer Street. One was considerably younger than the other. The older one smiled and approached me for some money.

I asked the older one, offering him whatever change remained from the purchase, to buy me the cigarettes and together we walked to the nearest store. The man, Patrick, had just turned twenty-two and was broad-shouldered and appeared physically fit. He and his younger brother – who by contrast was a quiet and cowering boy – had returned from a retreat in upstate New York. Patrick was handsome: he had cropped ash-brown hair, cutting cheekbones and was tall. It was only the smut that covered his cheeks and brow, the thick-tongued speech and the state of his clothing, fraying and sullied, that gave away the nature of his problems. I asked him about himself as we proceeded on our walk along Summer Street to a nearby 7-Eleven whose lights painted the tarmac outside in a lurid white light.

My brother and I are from Gloucester, Patrick began, *our parents still live there, right out on the coast, just beyond the city. You know it? It's beautiful there but there's not much to do.* He paused and turned back at his brother, who was leaning against the station wall, before eventually admitting to me, *We're trying to get back home.* Back from where? I asked myself. Why couldn't they get back home? What had happened between their parents and them that meant that these two young men were trying to find their way back home? What had led them to find themselves as dishevelled as they are now? And as our conversation continued, more questions flooded my mind. Why was it that their parents had refused contact with Patrick and banned him from their house? Why did Patrick talk with subtle traces of disgrace when he mentioned his parents? Was it that he thought of his father calling him *a sickening disgrace*? Or, *a stain on this family*? Or was it that he knew his parents felt threatened by him, much bigger than them both, as after an argument years ago now in a drug-addled rage, he reached for his father's gun – was that it, the final straw? Or was it that he knew they couldn't bear to look at him for what he'd turned their youngest son into? Or was it that like him, they felt an implacable pain each night when they thought of the time before then, and that they were forced to reflect on what in some way they felt responsible for? But that distance – that is ever-extending yet not as wide as we often feel it to be – helped them cope with their dreams, their terrors and the quieter times when one of them would stumble across a photo of their eldest and forgive him, deep within them, forgive him a thousand times but never in actuality permit themselves to; leaving them all, the two boys, the two parents, to instead walk the earth separated, divorced from each other but full of crumbling thoughts of the other, all only wishing that that distance they had cemented over time would one day collapse.

Our family run a landscaping business there, Patrick explained. *Over the summers, I would work it with my dad and uncle. In the evenings I'd go to football practice. My little brother wasn't sporty like me. I was always a sports player, you know, that's the way Dad wanted it*, he went on, clearing his throat, *even from when I was young, like five or six, I played football.*

Dad pushed me to do it. I wasn't too big on it at first, didn't really mind it much, but there wasn't much else going for me. I used to like doing landscaping: the pruning and gardening especially. I always said if I don't do football, I'll have my own landscaping business. When I got to Amherst, I was playing Division One and was doing good there, until my sophomore year when I broke my ankle pretty badly, snapped some ligaments and it was sorta rough for me from then. I was prescribed pills, Oxys, to deal with the pain. I finished my course and moved on to something stronger. Struck by his sincerity, his totally affectless words, I asked about his brother. *I was shooting up at my parents' house,* he explained, *in their basement. I don't know how. I don't remember too much if I'm honest. I don't like to. But my little brother got hooked too. He was fifteen at the time. Now he's worse than I am. I don't like to think about it if I'm honest.* After buying me the cigarettes, we walked back to his brother and each of us had one. The younger boy didn't speak but smiled with a beautiful and admiring timidity at whatever it was Patrick spoke of. I stayed with them until the conversation petered into silence then left them with my cigarettes.

After this encounter, whenever I would see an ambulance and Patricia would say, *There goes another one,* I would quietly believe it to be one of those two brothers, imagining one of them overdosing as though it was some cruel inevitability that had been fated by the blankness with which Patrick explained his tragedy to me. Making it seem that he knew before I did that death or near-death was to be the singular consequence of our encounter, that there was no use in systematizing a preventative strategy, that as far as he was concerned things were decided and simply barrelling, or dawdling, along to their unfussy end.

When I thought of it, I always imagined it to be Patrick first, but it was some months later that I saw a framed picture of his younger brother on a local news station, with the same self-effacing and quiet look I had seen in the dead of night outside South Station, held in the shaking hands of an inconsolable mother stood outside the gates of a pharmaceutical company, surrounded by a pack of sullen faces, young and old; a mother who couldn't help but feel the full and oppressive weight of responsibility that had, in the days and weeks since she heard her little boy had died, pinned her to her bed, leaving her to linger in a lifeless and thoughtless pain. A feeling that was too strong for her to give words to and too absolute to remain in silence over. She, from then, would live in that strange position I have found so many of us having lived – pressed between a piercing howl and an irreversible silence.

In between working at Les Sablons, I spent my hours in a Dunkin' Donuts tucked beneath a parking garage. There is something to be said for the anonymity conferred by franchise spaces as though it is the rigidity of their form, the immutability of their interior, that translates a similar kind of invisibility onto the passing faces that enter. I first experienced this sense in this Dunkin' Donuts, or at least became aware of it, as I found myself unthinking for a moment and comfortably unnoticed. For each second my body was asserted as it was, it was simultaneously waning in appearance until soon no eyes inspected me, no one cared, no one questioned my figure, no one scrutinized me. I was there, so present, so accepted and so unheeded, that just as much – I was not there. I remember explaining this feeling to Patricia excitably and her laughing at me. Embarrassedly I asked why she laughed and still chuckling she explained, *All I ever wanted was to be seen, to be heard.*

Patricia often complained to me about her job: *I'm gonna leave soon. I'm done with all that shit now*, but she never did. It seemed the more she spoke about it, the less her conviction to do it meant anything and each time I asked her why she continued to work as a bus driver despite loathing it, her face would drop and she'd hastily cobble together a different answer made up of the same old words.

We'd sometimes take long drives in her old grey Subaru around Boston and she'd sing croakily along to whatever played on WHBR, the smoke from her cigarette mixing with the cold Boston air, blustering specks of ash onto the back seat. Sometimes, we'd stop somewhere for coffee and she'd tell me about the cities that she wanted to visit. The one in particular she kept talking about was Edinburgh in Scotland. *I've seen photos of it*, she'd say, *I would love to go*, and assuming the role of worldly traveller that I felt she wanted of me I would tell her about the Royal Mile, spitting on the Heart of Midlothian where the Old Tollbooth had once stood and of the network of tunnels and vaults that run beneath the city. And she'd listen, quiet, still, sometimes with her eyes closed as I spoke, imagining herself there.

One evening, near the end of my time in Massachusetts, Patricia invited me over to dinner at hers, *I want you to see my boy.* She gave me her address and in the quiet north-eastern evening I arrived from off the Alewife Brook Parkway and stood at the foot of the three towers that I had once scowled at as a boy, once questioned and scrutinized, unravelled and undone in my head, in disgust or confusion. Patricia told me that she had lived there as long as she'd been in Boston. *When I first arrived, it was dangerous. I know it doesn't look it now, but back then it was dark everywhere. I remember junkies in the corridors, slumped in the stairwells. At night, you could always hear somebody hollering. Someone always had to be shouting about something. Someone getting beat or whatever. The whole place had a different feel to it. But no one cared. The police, the housing authority – no one. It was like we were invisible in these towers. Which is crazy because you can't ignore them, they're the tallest buildings around. Anyways, that doesn't matter. That's what I've learnt, it doesn't matter. No matter how tall, small, fat, wide or thin you are, you can still be invisible. And that's what this place was and the people who lived in it – unseen.*

The table was laid for three with a large dish of lasagne and a big bowl of salad. We began to talk and I waited for the third guest, but Patricia started on her food, so I joined in. *He's coming . . . He's coming,* she kept saying whenever I asked. The third guest never arrived. I stopped asking. After dinner, we sat in her brown carpeted living room, lit only by the glow of a naked bulb and a muted television which showed the news as Patricia told me about some of her experiences in the towers. As she spoke of her memories, she became increasingly apathetic and weary, as though each flicker of violence, tale of fear and single tear that welled in her eyes provoked a deep pain that till now she had prevented me from seeing, like giving words to the thing renewed its reality.

One such story I can recall in particular was of a boy she watched be stabbed to death from her window. She told me of the flurry of shadowed figures floors below her as she pressed the phone to her ear to call the police. The words and images that she thought of caused her eyes to widen. *It looked like a dance from up here*, and required her to prop herself up on the couch when telling it to me. *It was crazy*, but as she spoke and explained it, I noticed her eyes couldn't meet mine. *I ran down to help*, and this became so evident that I realized she was intentionally avoiding them. *I didn't know who it was*, as if to catch sight of my face would cause her to cry.

From the eighteenth floor you could see all across Cambridge, right down to the Boston skyline, which the Prudential Center and the blue glass of 200 Clarendon Street dominated. As the sun slowly set, the shape of those buildings drew out into large vertical shadows on the land below. From the other side, you could see Fresh Pond perfectly. I imagined seeing it in winter, looking down onto the skaters. I thought of that old Dutch painting that still hangs in the Rijksmuseum and

I wondered what Avercamp might have made of the distending cityscape from this vanishing height.

For the remainder of the night, Patricia spoke in a whispered voice. *They didn't do anything about it. It wasn't in the papers, on television, no one was ever arrested, no one ever knew. It felt like me alone.* I drifted off into thought looking at the glinting lights of the city below. When I went to the bathroom, I noticed a room with its door ajar and the light on behind it. Peeking through, I saw a single bed, perfectly set, the room exquisitely maintained, the books were as I imagined they always had been, sets of shoes were under the bed and pyjamas were perfectly folded on top of the duvet. When I returned, Patricia was asleep, and only then did I notice the huge spread of photos of her son that covered the walls around the television. There was a black-and-white photograph of two people, a young boy nestled into the bosom of a young Patricia on a street corner. I took it in my hand and on the back of it, in archival ink was written: *Jesse and me, NYC.* From his neck hung the same canted gold head she wore but this time it faced me. In all the photos, she was smiling as I hadn't ever seen her smile before.

As she slept, I watched the view of the city disappear into darkness until it seemed that the clusters of houselights across Cambridge and Boston were constellations of stars. My eyes fell upon the exact point in the parking lot of Fresh Pond from which I had looked up at the building I now occupied and again my grandmother's words returned to me, much as these very towers had too, *For people to live in.* Patricia was still asleep. I left her with a blanket over her and two weeks later, after finishing work, I returned to my mother's home in Oxford.

Two years later, I received an email from the executor of Patricia's will, a cousin of hers. She had passed away of lung cancer. He wanted to know what my address was in order to send what it was that Patricia had left me. I was surprised to know she had left me anything at all as we had hardly stayed in touch since I had left. But some weeks later, my mother came to my bedroom door and handed me a package. She stood in the door frame and watched me open it. Inside was a full bottle of her perfume – '1000' by Jean Patou – and a scribbled note to me that I won't share the contents of. Upon first seeing the perfume, my mother said in slight shock, *I used to wear that perfume.* And as though latent and lain dormant, deep at the ends of my body, a great burst of emotion coursed through me. I still cling to the thought Patricia sensed of the rising of childhood memories in me the first time I met her. I thought of her life, of her son, Jesse: two of the forgotten, left to die as they lived – unseen and unheard.

In 1979, a boy just thirteen years old was driven through the night from a hospital in Slough to a small apartment in Little Venice. The boy's father had bought it, as well as the smaller separate unit above, some five years earlier and until then both spaces had been used solely for storage. When they arrived, the apartments – just as they were when I first visited years later – were filled with an assortment of unopened boxes, antique furniture covered in heavy white sheets and a thick dust lolling in the airless space. As the sleeping boy's aunt held him, his father and mother opened the windows, releasing the dust and heat into the cold black air. They removed the sheets from the furniture and made up a bed for him in the living room. The boy's grandmother arrived within the hour in a long raincoat, clasping seven dried red chillies to her chest. She sat beside the sleeping boy, and under the expectant gaze of her son-in-law and her two daughters, she mixed salt and mustard seeds together and sprinkled them across the feverish and naked chest of her grandson, Sulli. She then softly dragged each chilli across his body from head to toe as she whispered a prayer that warded off dark spirits. When she was done, the grandmother was sent home in a cab. The boy's father and mother set up a bed in the attic unit. The boy's aunt Jedha remained lain at his side, watching him through the night, praying he would recover.

The young boy, Sulli, the son of a wealthy Indian business-man, was found to have water on the brain after suffering an epileptic fit in his dormitory at his school in Windsor. He was discovered by his housemaster, Mr Dow, a portly Welshman who smelt of pipe tobacco and whose stomach pressed against his jacket buttons like the burl of an oak tree. When Mr Dow found the boy convulsing on the carpet, he quickly rushed him to hospital. The boy spent several weeks receiving treat-ment with his mother and Aunt Jedha beside him, both praying without pause from morning till twilight.

His aunt took up a room at the nearby Sir Christopher Wren Hotel, as at night she liked to sit on the riverside and watch people cross the bridge just like she had done years before when living in Paris and looking at the empty niches of the Pont Marie, enjoying the absence of memorial in a city otherwise diffuse with it. The boy's mother remained at his bedside, only leaving to shower in her sister's hotel room or to eat what little she could manage. The boy's treatment was concluded with hydrocephalus: the attachment of a drainage tube from his head down to his stomach. The shunt alleviated the pressure that the build-up of the fluid had created but did little to offset the damage the pressure had silently caused and by the time the boy was carried up to bed in Little Venice he had already suffered neurological damage.

I met Sulli the summer after returning from Boston, when I stumbled across an advertisement for a garret posted on a listings board for a suspiciously reasonable price; a price that made it seem that the person renting it didn't truly require any money from the rental. I rode my father's bike to Little Venice, stopping briefly in Rembrandt Gardens before continuing to 32 Blomfield Road to meet the landlord of the garret, Sulli. I pushed the bike through the black wrought-iron gate into the leaf-covered drive and rang the bell for Flat 2. The upper windows and their trimmings were blanketed in a charcoal grime and peeling paint beneath the pristinely kept lower windows. Even the bell for Flat 2 I noticed was yellowing and without a name tag compared to the other apartment's sections. As I found myself inspecting the grand building, quickly and uneasily, a short man wearing a ragged hunting jacket peeked his balding head round the door and sharply barked, *Come.* He appeared unwashed and his eyes were reddened by what seemed a lack of sleep. The man rushed off ahead of me without a further word. I rested my bicycle in the hall and arrived behind him rather unsteadily at an open red door through which floated the burning smell of saffron and bergamot. Sulli began then (and only then) busily cleaning up his apartment: *Take that sheet off there would you,* he ordered, pointing to what was obviously a veiled chair. I complied, folding the sheet and dragging it opposite to the walnut rocking chair that was by a window before taking a seat. *Tea? Coffee?* Sulli asked. I requested tea.

The curtains in the flat were all drawn bar one which permitted some of the day's remaining sun into the room. By the window was a steel ashtray filled with old butts and pocked with black marks beside a hastily lit stick of incense. The parqueted flooring was covered with old boxes dirtied with scum from years of smoke and dust. The kitchen was still fitted with its original plastic gas cooker which was equally as jaundiced as the pallid walls around it. The kettle shakily whistled, and Sulli soon brought over two cups of tea. The sun was covered by a cloud and the room darkened, contracting in size.

Sulli took a seat in his rocking chair, and in relative silence we sipped at our piping tea. I noticed resting on some boxes beside the kitchen a number of postal tubes. I asked Sulli what was in them and with a sigh he ran over to them and pulled out two prints of Velazquez paintings: one a portrait of Francisco Lezcano and the other of Sebastián de Morra. *I believe the Spanish artists*, he began to orate, *were the best. The best*, he repeated firmly. *There isn't a doubt about it in my mind. Goya, Velazquez, Zurbarán, all of them. The best*, he reaffirmed before asking me, *What're your thoughts on them?* And then, after a short pause he added, *You might not be intelligent enough to understand what I mean.* He later would explain to me that these provocative and cruel remarks, while rude, were the result of the damage that had been inflicted upon him as a child. After his seizure, he began to suffer from a total inability to filter himself and could not stop talking once you had him started. His mouth rushed on with his mind as though his mouth were his way of thinking. It was like he suffered from a total inability to think within the confines of his mind and required a kind of phoneticized cognition to disentangle his thoughts. This inevitably led to impulsive and insulting comments being made, despite him not entirely intending them to be so. These comments, I would later learn, had had him barred from every pub and restaurant within a mile of his apartment. He told me that he was barred from his local pub, The Warwick Castle, on his eighteenth birthday because when he went to order his first drink he asked the woman serving him what the size of her chest was in centimetres. No doubt, this was not derived of perversion but out of genuine biological curiosity and a total unawareness of certain social codes. On the night of his eighteenth, he left the pub without a drink and was unable to ever visit the pub again, and even despite many years having had passed since his being banned he never returned because of his shame.

In answer to his question, I had in fact seen these paintings some years before at the Prado Museum when I had visited Madrid with an old partner of mine, and after an afternoon spent arguing in the botanical garden I stormed into the museum and soon found myself stood in front of both these portraits, having forgotten what the reason we began arguing had been. But my mentioning this to Sulli landed dully and he continued as though I hadn't answered his question at all. *You aren't listening to me, are you? The seventeenth and eighteenth centuries in Spain were periods unrivalled in artistic production. Think of the vast amounts of original works created: 'Don Quixote', the plays of Tirso, Carbonell's 'Buen Reitro', which now you can only see sketches of. It goes on. I've often asked myself why it was in this general period that Spain found itself the creator of such seminal cultural and artistic work.* Sulli continued in this manner for close to half an hour without interruption, weighing up the inward social effects of war and the extensive expansion of the Spanish empire before finally his thought and torrent of words lapsed at the touch of his cold tea. Sulli made himself another then asked me to help him pin up the prints of the two Velazquez dwarves, and after nearly two hours of him talking through the paintings and rambling about other things such as his favourite flavour of crisp (Tyrrells' Salt and Vinegar) and the city that had the best moules-frites (Antwerp), he at last led me up to the garret that I hoped to rent from him.

It was dark and smaller than I expected it to be. Sulli led the way and pulled apart the heavy velvet curtains, allowing the light to bleed into the space like the diffusion of a dye in water, touching nooks and depths that seemingly retreated further and further under the eye of daylight. It became so bright so suddenly that I winced. Sulli began to move the boxes aside to create room for me to walk through. As I inspected the garret, Sulli left and went back downstairs. The apartment was tiny. The living area was attached to the kitchen in which the counters and stove top were also covered with piles of old pots, crockery, boxes of utensils and wooden crates filled with early era electronic appliances. The bedroom, which was to the right of the front door, contained a low-lying frame and mattress that was littered with stacks of papers and empty hangers. The hanging bulbs were exposed and didn't work and two switch panels were missing, leaving holes in the walls and exposed wiring.

Sulli returned moments later with several photographs, some framed and others not. He handed them to me one by one without prompt and began explaining what each one showed. *This one is of my father and my uncle. They're both from the Amritsar, Punjab. Behind them there is the Harmandir Sahib. They're extremely religious, my family. Proper loons about it, even after living here for so long. My father came here in 1950 and worked as a porter in an asylum in Norfolk. Rubbish job, that; he hated it but did it for a few years before moving to London to stay with his brother, and once he was there they opened a convenience store on Old Ford Road out east. In the evening, my father worked as a bus driver on the number 339, and in the morning he'd open the shop. He worked seven days a week, all day. This photo is of my mother and her sister; they're from Baluchistan. You see they're stood in front of Sacré-Coeur in Paris, about twenty-something-years-old each. I bet you wouldn't believe it was my mother's family that was affluent not my father's. Her family in Pakistan were rich merchants and of a higher caste but to her it didn't matter. She shunned all of that; she was very religious and spent all her time praying. She is always listening, a quiet woman, even now. I remember seeing her at dinners watching everything and everyone dance around her. When I think of her, she is like an angel because of this. She lives in the countryside now. I don't see her much. She is very old. Her sister, my aunt Jedha, was the opposite: a Europhile and a great talker like she had Irish in her or something.*

Sulli spoke with the drone of received pronunciation but also, at times, his parents' native accent was revealed, puncturing the flatness of his regular speech with higher-peaking sounds that shot off his tongue. His gaze was thorough: both intense and disinterested, like the subject of his scrutiny was, to him, of nothing more than fleeting interest. And the intensity of his glare, unmoving from your eyes, seemed only to be there to pierce the fat and once through it scoured only for weakness, for fragility.

I don't know how to describe my father, Sulli explained. *He's a silent bully. He doesn't speak much, not even to me. That's my punishment or his punishment for me. That's what he said once. He has worked pretty much his entire life. It's just work that he has. In the early 1960s, he and my uncle opened the first twenty-four-hour convenience store in London under their brand Old Ford's. They then developed this into their own brand of cash and carries which led to a huge boom in business for them. With more investment, they opened more twenty-four-hour stores across the country and as I always say, because of the winos and the students — like that! This all turned into a massive business empire that has been due to pay dividends to me for many years. I have the papers, the contracts, everything to prove it. I'm not lying, I can show you!* Sulli, suddenly silent and seemingly exasperated then abruptly and without any consideration for his sudden outburst, began to show me more photographs, one of which was of his aunt Jedha, his mother's sister. He took this photo out of the pile and pocketed it quickly.

After nearly four hours with Sulli, two prints hung up and an entire case of photographs leafed through, I agreed to take the apartment upstairs. Two weeks later, when I arrived again with a suitcase and a box, the apartment had not been touched since I had first visited, and Sulli was sat in his special rocking chair, smoking and laughing madly at an old copy of *A Sentimental Journey*. I spent the first week of my stay helping Sulli clear out my apartment: moving boxes into a storage space downstairs and dusting corners and edges that had been left uncleaned for years, all as Sulli continually tried to tell me Sterne's story of 'The Dead Ass' in Nampont but found himself unable to through fits of laughter that came with each attempt.

I spent much of my stay there with Sulli, either in his apartment or with him in mine. He would typically allow himself into the garret without knocking or asking. I quickly became familiar with all manners of his affairs with his family who had, according to him, forced him to remain cooped up in this apartment as they continued their work on the family business. His father would only contact him to tell him to remain out of sight, out of the way of the business and away from any prying media that were interested in the estranged and reclusive son of the multi-millionaire immigrant family.

The more Sulli and I spoke, the more it became apparent to me that his family (his father, in particular) saw his illness and the seizure he suffered as a boy to be the work of the devil or some intangible mystic evil. Because of this it was decided among the men in the family that he should be kept hidden away. *He'd always tell me I had the evil eye on me from birth,* Sulli explained. *And ever since I had that seizure, he treated me like I planned to enact some devilry on my own family. It's crazy and paranoid!*

Despite the clear difficulty and strain he felt between himself and his family, Sulli often spoke of his aunt Jedha more gently but, in truth, he never disclosed more about her to me than the odd memory from his childhood. His tone when speaking of her was markedly different from the one he composed of his father. It was softer, sweeter, desolate in some places and consoled in others, as though when he conjured her using only words, the images that he returned to were so whole and perfectly contoured that he was back within them as he recalled them. Naturally, I imagined, Sulli was aware of his family's fear of him, and while he did little to alter his wholly *comfortable* situation, he often, following a rambling tirade of words, tended to return to his melancholic refrain, *I only want to be free.* It was in those moments that Sulli appeared to me as caged and confined, as constricted and alone as he truly was.

One night as it snowed outside, the two of us ate dinner together in his apartment and Sulli spoke of something in him I hadn't heard amid the noise of his usual patter. After our meal, he curtly rose and began rummaging through an unsealed box that was obscured in the corner of the room beside the window he smoked out of. He took out a thick collection of crumbling papers with a precision that indicated he had undertaken this action countless times and began to thumb through them, sheet by sheet. *Jedha's letters,* he uttered. As Sulli thumbed meticulously through the letters, he spoke to me. *My aunt lived in Paris when she was a young woman. She studied there and quickly she fell in love with the city and a woman named Josephine. For years, she hid their relationship from our family. She was worried she would disgrace them with her sexuality. Also, because she was scared that they might force her to leave Paris. But after several years spent together, and at a healthy distance from her family, my aunt's security and confidence cemented in her and she felt enough courage to reveal her partner to our family. My mother once explained to me that upon hearing this news, my grandfather became sheet white and very calm and said very quietly, 'She is beyond help so let her go. Let her wander further off but when she returns, she should know there is no promise we will be here waiting,' and at that point, without even so much as a second thought, my grandfather made the decision on behalf of the family to break all ties with her. This decision caused my grandmother tremendous pain and was what my mother and father believe brought her to an early and unexpected death at the age of forty-nine. Even with this embargo in place – yes, I call it an embargo – my grandmother and my mother both remained in touch with Jedha throughout but they never made a point of it in front of anyone. They kept their contact with her a secret, even though everyone knew that they were doing it.* Sulli explained to me that as the family and Jedha grew further apart, so did the contact they kept with her become more minimal. Till soon, the erasure of Jedha's image from living memory was almost total, almost complete.

One night, he continued, *in 1980, Josephine went to visit a friend for a birthday dinner in Chaville, a small suburb of Paris. And as she was driving back at around midnight, on what were mostly empty roads, a drunk driver lost control of his car and swerved into hers. The impact killed her immediately.* Sulli paused for a moment and furrowed his brows, as if still confused at what he was about to say. *And after this happened, Jedha began to lose a hold on her sense of the world.* He then paused again before saying, *My mother, my grandmother, stopped hearing from their sister, their daughter. Jedha began to blame them for it. She would leave calls and send threatening letters without a name at their house, accusing them of wild conspiracies like: her father had hired the man to swerve into Josephine's car to kill her, or that Josephine wasn't really dead but had been paid by her family to disappear. Jedha would often call the family home screaming repeatedly, 'Where is she?! Where did you send her?!' She even began to believe that her sister was somehow a part of the plan, which hurt my mother immensely.* Sulli explained that gradually these crazed theories outwardly subsided but Jedha inwardly harboured the same suspicions right up until the end of her life.

Of course, Sulli said and cleared his throat, *it was the logic of grief. But this kind of behaviour continued over the course of the year until one night she was found wandering down the roads of Montrouge screaming at people who were sat on the balcony of Josephine's old apartment. She was barking threats and abuse up at them and was eventually approached by two police*

officers. When one officer asked her, 'What's the fucking issue?'
And ordered her to 'Be quiet, you crazy old cow', Jedha, blind
with rage, struck him once then twice. She was quickly thrown
to the floor and arrested on the spot. Two years later, when the
bastards did finally psychiatrically evaluate her, they realized
she was suffering from an episode of reactive psychosis and she
was committed to a psychiatric hospital located in the fourteenth
arrondissement.

At last, Sulli landed upon the letter he was looking for,
and he carefully removed what looked like a scan of a letter
from a blank envelope with a delicacy and dexterity he'd not
displayed before. He then opened it and scanned its contents
before reading it aloud to me:

23/03/84

Dearest Sulli,

Thank you for yours. It's always such a delight to hear
from you. Nowadays, I hear little, if anything at all, from
anyone. I last received mail from your mother six months
ago. It is not that I am upset by this, it is just that I feel
I've been forgotten.

Being forgotten was always a great fear of mine. So much
so, as a young girl I felt the need to engrave my name on
every object, every possession I owned, to the point that my
father would beat me with a belt because I had scratched
my name into the leather of the couch or used a knife to

carve my name into the dining table. Even in books that weren't my own, I would write my name as I was comforted by the idea that if I were one day to disappear, someone, even if they didn't know me at all, would have seen my name, my handwriting and have wondered, even briefly, of its originator. This odd hope was my comfort as I sensed through it, I could never be forgotten.

But now, even after just two years here, I fear the ink I had used has since faded, the etchings I made into bits of wood have been sanded off and the leather of the sofa re-upholstered. Maybe, as I have come to think, I am gone in other's minds and in the world, and as that is, I don't truly exist anymore. I have been forgotten. It is only your letters that have so far warded off these thoughts. For which, I thank you. There is nothing worse than nothingness.

I wish I was able to come and see your face and your wide hazel eyes. I fear that I won't make it long enough in here to do so again. I am filled with thoughts that I will never be able to leave here. By no means am I allowed out of the hospital grounds, not even with a nurse. It is hellish. So I think of the various patients who have also been here: your beloved Celan, the great painter Delaney among others, and I feel in good company with the spirits of great minds, their echoes, although faint, resound clearly enough to keep me sane.

I am warmed by what you say of your wanting to go back to school to complete your studies. I feel such pain thinking of your situation. I agree that it is time you continue your

*education. Come to Paris. It was a wonderful time studying
here for me.*

*But my dear Sulli, enough now. When you become afraid
think of the words Beckett spoke to Bram van Velde after
the war:*

Bram says, 'Oh, I haven't seen you for years, Sam.'
Beckett replies with an embrace, 'Only physically.'

J.

Sulli carefully slipped the letter back into its place then
thumbed forward and took out another. He looked at it for a
moment, his eyes unmoving, and suddenly, as mechanically
as he had the first, he began to read it:

19/10/93

*I have not heard from you for some time and have been
worried sick that you too have forgotten me. I sometimes
think about your mother and even your father. But always
about my dear Jo. I cannot escape her; she refuses to leave
me. Things have changed little here although I have begun
to feel myself growing old. An odd feeling. My heart, of
course, is still young.*

*They have moved me to a room with a view of the
garden. In it there are beautiful statues and the birds twit
and talk to each other. It is peaceful enough. Much better
than the room before, beside which a poor woman called
Calypso wept day and night without end about a son she
never had.*

I wish you too could see the statues so I could hear what you think of them.

J.

Again, Sulli put the page away and took out another. On the bottom-right corner of the page, I noticed a smudge of inky thumbprints, indelible black marks, revealing years of reading and re-reading. The next letter Sulli read slower and with a certain degree of reluctance:

23/02/94

The other day, as I was watching night fall across the grounds, the statues gave the grave impression of vibrating, of pulsing with movement. I felt they were moving, dancing, howling and living beneath me. I felt they were freer than me. Away my mind ran with this idea and so much so I began to believe they were communing and meditating together with the spirits of Celan and Delaney and the rest. They seemed at times to look at me, to turn to my window and urge me to join them but the bars on the window wouldn't allow for it.

By then, it was too dark to see. I can hear the streets outside.

The other night, I dreamt I saw your father in my room, he was talking to me about you and weeping. He was telling me things, shouting at me. I screamed and woke up. Seconds later, the echo of a pistol shot rang out. There was a great commotion. Our rooms were searched. We were all taken to the common room, herded like cattle in the dead of night into a communal hall then sent back to bed hours later.

I found out that one of the patients – Mahmood, who to me, resembled your father – had smuggled in a pistol and shot himself with it. I became too nervous to sleep. I feel I have, in some odd way, caused the poor soul's death.

I have allowed these fears to spiral in me so much that they have broken ground on new anxieties, ones I didn't even know I could have. My only method of stopping them has been to return to a memory of something. I recorded some of the recollections that have soothed me on the enclosed paper.

J.

Sulli put the letter to one side and sighed. Eventually, after some time sat together in silence, he took out the scrap of paper that was folded within the letter. He held it in his shaking hand and his gaze softened ever so slightly. He explained before opening it: *I should tell you that when Aunt Jedha was committed to Sainte-Anne they instantly deemed her as posing a risk of self-harm and so put her on suicide watch. Do you know what they do to those patients who are on this? They intensely surveil them: hourly checks and regular and invasive searches of their room and cavities. As well as this, they aren't able to use towels to shower and she wasn't able to change into her single piece, tear-resistant suit without being watched by a nurse. If she acted out of manner, they'd restrain her with buckles and leather. She was systematically degraded and reduced to nothing more than a flightless bird, a butterfly without wind. And in the twelve years she was there,* he went on with a seething anger in his words, *I was the only one to write or speak to her, the only one to keep in any contact with her. The rest of my family? They ignored her, did well to forget her. They did forget her! They went on with their lives without a thought for her! In my family, her absence was filled with bullshit news and talk of minuscule change: children, business, studies and the gradual so on and so forth of life. And all the while their daughter, their sister, their niece, their aunt was alone, isolated, in a tiny lockable room far away from them.* His face, incensed and pulsing, slowly unscrewed and loosened and he returned to looking mournfully out onto the dark road.

That was until, he said softly, *at the age of forty-nine, one morning, she was found hanged in her room. The nurse found her facing the garden with the window slightly open, just enough for her to hear the birdsong.*

Sulli remained in silence for some time. He poured himself a large splash of wine before resuming his position by the window. He took out a cigarette and stared onto Regent's Canal. The scintillant water under the snowy night filled his mind with images of the Seine's creased black water, the same water his aunt recounted to him with such fondness. He didn't light the cigarette. His body froze to a sculptural stillness. The last few remaining images and thoughts, feelings and otherwise, crackled and withdrew in him like gasping coals in a fire pit. He shivered a little at the cold wind coming through the window but remained distant, looking out onto the water and onto the houses; onto the cars and road signs that he'd bothered with his attention for years and recognized with both familiarity and still, after all this time, a certain hatred, as he too had been confined his entire life, and these sights were no more than the shadows in his cave. In that moment, as he had done many times before, he felt a deep tension twang between him and his aunt Jedha like they were conjoined across time, space and death by no more than rusting piano wire, and this tension, this thrum, was one of harmony not discordance, as they were the same prisoner only in different prisons.

As I watched him there, I thought of the words that returned to him in moments like these, the words marked with echoes of freedom, of an inescapable desire for something, anything else entirely, and the want that pinched at him when the earth felt at its most contracted. He was as inconsolable as his aunt as she was swaddled into a navy smock and as fearing as his unblinking mother when she lay in the hospital in Slough watching her sleeping son with a shunt running down from his head to his stomach.

He was both of them then.

It could've been any amount of time until either of us spoke again. Still now, I am unsure who spoke first. Sat back in his chair with only his silhouette visible in the moonlight, Sulli read to me the final words he received from his aunt Jedha:

Do you remember? If you think back far enough, is what emerges all there was? Or has the rest vanished like it never was? The question is not what, but if. It is simple enough, J. I have thought about it and see how all my memory is eaten away and ravaged not by what I've forgotten but what I've remembered. What I want to know about is that which seems gone now. And what is there is
of no use to me.

When we were younger, my sister Sabah and I would travel together with our cousin to Hingol Park from our family home in Karachi. We would hike across the hills and swim at Kund Malir, deep into the clear and wide sea. On these travels, we would bring the food our Dadi would prepare for us and if it was the season we'd bring mangoes, slice and eat them in the sand. Our cousin, if the sun fell early, would park his truck at the water's edge and switch on the headlights. We would sit in the car and watch the water break under the glow of the lights.

Once, on a walk along the flatlands in the park, we spotted a man cloaked in long white robes with a cedar wood stick. He approached us and spoke to my cousin. The man revealed to us that he was a Sufi sheikh. He said only a few words to us, all with a slight and knowing smile. We offered him water and food to take with him, but he refused. He had no need for it. The beating sun sank behind a fold in the land. In the shadow it cast we stood with nothing and no one else around us. Before the sheikh continued on his way, he turned to me, took my hand, looked deeply into me, sensing something, and asked, 'Daughter, what is it you are withholding from the sky?'

In the first months I studied in Paris, before I knew anyone there, I spent much of my time alone. I would take long walks some days and sleep endlessly for others. One day, when taking my usual walk from the Latin Quarter to the Palais Garnier, I found I had managed to end up just beyond my usual destination, all without my realizing. I ended up some ten minutes north at Sainte-Trinité. A vesper service had just finished, and as a trickle of people spilled out onto the street I sidled into the emptying church. I sat near the back and marvelled for some time at the interlocking, geometric stain-glass work: cerise interlaced with dark blue. The church was so extremely beautified, so overly ornate, I felt myself lessening beneath its heft. I felt reduced into something so small and so insignificant. I was calmed. I felt small. I felt free.

I don't quite remember what distraction had caused me to make that mistake. But in making it, I landed upon something that quelled whatever anxiety had fluttered inside of me that day. The embers of incense from the thurible glowed; its smoke continued to drift from its silver.

Sat there, I found myself thinking back to the mystic dragging himself on through the barren land, and suddenly, as though miraculously, I saw myself between two worlds; an odd chassis folded by the weight of the twin landscapes within me that I had desperately pushed apart. It is these two thoughts, these two memories, that I continue to think

*of when I want equipoise. I am not sure why. I don't
interrogate the feeling much as my mind tries to. I ignore
myself. I sit in meditation with the images and figures that
appear in that silence.*

Sulli explained his deep regret at what had happened to his
aunt and confessed of the anger he felt towards his mother
and father for the way in which they treated her, saying to
me, *When one treats their own family in this way, it begs the
question who else could they treat as badly?* After this, I shared
the cigarette with Sulli in silence, and as I stumbled to return
to my apartment he asked me, *What do you think then? Is there
any way any of us can be free?* Without allowing time for an
answer, he closed the door behind me. I can still remember
the sound of him humming loudly as I stumbled up the stairs
to bed.

I stayed in Little Venice for just over a year. At least once
a week, Sulli and I would talk together in his apartment,
exchanging slivers of news or any personal developments, and
occasionally he'd ask me to help with some moving in his
apartment. But never again did we converse as intimately as
we did that night. The more I settled into the garret of
32 Blomfield Road, the more those moments of exchange
between us waned. Sulli began to see more of his parents as
his mother grew ill and increasingly spent time away from his
home in London. It was three years after I moved out, having
had next to no communication with him after my leaving,
that I spotted Sulli walking happily down the road with

another man's hand interlaced within his own. He smiled and continued walking, without a word.

As the years passed and I myself travelled through the world, on certain nights or certain days when there were stray moments, those loose and floating enough for reflection, I'd find the words of Jedha's letters resounding in me. She was a woman that despite never knowing, I had formed such a clear conception of. I had always been struck by that. I felt, in truth, I had no right to contain such a vivid image of a woman I'd only heard spoken of through the words of her embittered and lonely nephew. And my understanding (and misunderstanding) of her simmered within me for years until one night when I was staring aimlessly out of my window, watching twilight swallow the world as a starry and falling snow delicately began to dust the black roads, I began to parse through files on my computer to declutter it. Amid the junk, in a file lazily labelled 'Old', I found a scan of the poem that my mother would read to me as a boy. I clicked on the file and for the first time in years I read through it before quickly reading it again and again. And each time as I finished the poem, I found it was no longer my mother that came to mind, or rather, not my mother alone, but the image of Jedha and the image of Sulli, both of them alongside the image of the prisoner-poet.

After this, I emailed Sulli the poem, despite it having been many years since we'd last spoken. I received a response from him several weeks later – an email without a subject or words,

only the scan of a page from one of Jedha's journals that she
kept when she was a student in Paris:

30/11/65

*I woke up late this morning, far beyond the time I usually
do. I put this down, as I told Willa* [her flatmate at the
time] *to the horrible dreams I have been having recently.
Usually, my nights are dreamless or forgotten. I don't know
which one is truer. But in the past few days, my dreams
have been disturbing. So disturbing that I find myself in the
same frozen shock hours after I wake up.*

*Willa and I walked down to a nearby café where we ate.
While she went off to class, leaving me to wander the area,
I went to an old antique shop beside the café and picked up
a slim collection of decadent poetry and a copy of 'Journal
Intime' by Amiel. I bought them both for four Francs and
walked home afterward.*

Across the remainder of the page, Jedha had written out,
in meticulous, almost machine-like script, a number of
lines from poems she particularly liked from the collection.
Throughout the yellowed and ink-stained page, she had
scrawled hastily single words like 'sails' and vague pairs like
'tumultuous night', 'lover's gloaming' and 'wandering lost'.
Beneath these, however, out of the margins of the lined paper
and half-hidden by a heavy blot of India ink were the following words circled repeatedly:

There is a pit of shame,
And in it lies a wretched man
Eaten by teeth of flame,
In burning winding-sheet he lies,
And his grave has got no name.

Again, without fail, there it was staring back at me. This time on the scan of a loose, crumbling page that had once been a part of a set of notebooks that in the intervening years the author's nephew, my onetime landlord, had scoured religiously each night with a dim lamp like an old religious hermit poring over ancient prayers. He'd read the text so finely and scrupulously so as not to miss a single word that might indicate something to him: a hesitation, the expansion of ink from a halted pen, the abatement of breath, or sentences that would indicate the wild unfurling of feeling (take for instance, *She looked so beautiful in that grey light that I knew I couldn't resist her*). In his aunt's writing he was not looking for an answer from her or even some clue or final and irrefutable answer that would soothe his perennial confusions about her life and inwardly his own. Instead, he was seeking a presence: the presence of his beloved aunt that he felt on the quieter days was absent and fading slowly and softly in him. And so each night, to hush that aching void he'd read her words repeatedly on the page so that on quieter days he'd hear her voice, smell her bergamot perfume and the old sense of her, the smiling and warm student, the adventurous and free soul, was revealed in him as vivid and as ravaged as ships and cityscapes emerging through the sea spray of old masters' paintings, and he was consoled, as through her he understood himself and through understanding her – he became free.

And as always, circling and vulturous, when I read the poem the words came accompanied with the slight and feeble memory that I still stored of my mother beside me on the edge of utter darkness, singing the words of the prisoner, the solitary and longing prisoner, in a voice both softer and gentler than I last remembered.

There is a black-and-white photograph of me as a child that was taken at the wake of my godfather. It shows me dressed in a boxy black suit, sat alone, staring wide-eyed and perplexed back at the camera. The flash trims my pupils with a thin white ring and my dark lips are slightly set apart in surprise. The swollen bridge of my recently broken nose protrudes unnaturally at a harsh, diagonal angle, as my thick wiry hair hides a slick of sweat perspiring from my brow. I recall when I was first shown the picture by my father, I was so embarrassed that I hid all traces of it from myself and my family. I remember, however, despite my youthful insecurity, it being a picture my father adored of me and one that he went so far as to obtain a copy of directly from the friend who took it to hang in his home. I can still recall my horror when going to visit my father in London from my mother's home in Oxford the year after they separated, and for the first time being presented with my enormous pre-pubescent and ill-formed face on the wall of his new apartment. I cried out and ran to tear it down but my disgust quickly dissipated when my father revealed to me that the reason he liked that picture of me so much was because it allowed him to think of his dear late friend, my godfather, indirectly.

As my father moved from country to country, from London, to Switzerland, to France and to Oman – that restless tendency of his being a part of the reason for my parents' separation – the picture disappeared with him each time, and in those years of not seeing him I forgot about its existence entirely. After my father passed away in 2018, three years before my mother to the day, I found the picture beneath a heap of coats and boxes in his studio apartment in West London. The glass of the frame had shattered and the corners of the picture were slightly scratched by the shards. But as time would have it, the highly defined face I had once felt immense disgust in looking at remained perfectly intact. I spent that afternoon alone in my father's home and can recall sitting on the sofa, staring at the picture for quite some time. What initially began as a reflection into my boyish insecurities at the time quickly turned into faltering attempts to remember the wake at which it was taken, the funeral before and the man who it was all for.

I began tracing what I remembered of my godfather's funeral, which was held late one March when I was no older than thirteen. It had been just three years since my parents' separation, and in that time I hadn't seen my father once and so I felt a certain distance from him and his life. Still, without a say in it, my father dressed me in a borrowed suit and a hastily knotted tie to accompany him. The funeral was held at Kensal Green Cemetery whose thawing grounds, along with the attendees, were recovering from the wintry nadir of February. I arrived in a taxi with my father, who, other than to offer the destination and to thank the driver as we exited, had remained morbidly silent throughout the drive. Hand in hand, we approached the milling cortège and quickly my father's silence gave way to a consolatory but bewildered voice that would last for many months after.

I recall walking from the entrance to the chapel, finding myself alone and uneasily winding behind a line of weary and baffled mourners. I didn't recognize anyone in the distant gaggle, and in that moment I – for a reason I can't be sure of – felt fearful of them. Unsure how to behave or how to present myself to the bereaved adults, with diffidence, I avoided them. I safely pocketed my hands and shunned their sullen and weepy gazes. I learned then to feign disinterest in order to escape the shame I felt at the thought of presenting no feeling to those who so deeply and painfully felt. As I know now, without quite realizing it then, I was trailing in the wake of a vast and varied history from which I was both excluded and included, a part of and separate from, knowing of and yet unmistakably and immovably ignorant of.

After finding the photograph and being struck by the inveterate gap in my memory of my godfather, I asked my mother for details about him. She told me his name was Max Mitnick, and explained his close relationship to my father, which began as two young and outcast boys at school and continued into their adult life, wherefrom Max became absent from my father too soon, who then too became absent from me too soon. I pressed my mother to tell me more about Max and my father's friendship but, for some reason (tiredness, perhaps?) she didn't want to say anything more and our conversation on him seemed to end just as soon as it had begun. This silence persisted until the following summer, when my mother called to tell me Max's father, Adam, had passed away at the age of eighty-six. She had received the news from a close family friend of the Mitnicks, a woman who had known my father and mother when they were younger. Curious and troubled by the diaphanous idea I held of Max, I asked my mother for the woman's phone number. That same day, I called and an elderly sounding woman answered over a crackling line. Her name was Margaret, she was an artist and a close family friend of the Mitnicks, and since Adam's recent passing she had been left to clear out the Mitnick family home in Stockwell. We talked for several minutes; I explained who I was and what my interest in speaking to her was and by the end of our brief conversation I had agreed to meet her at her home in the Norfolk countryside in a week's time.

On my day of travel, the sky was clear blue and warm. The air around Liverpool Street Station was filled only with the faraway and occasional hum of passing planes. The city streets, steeped in the day's heat, were unusually empty and quiet. The timing of my ticket to Norwich meant that my carriage was mostly empty. After leaving London, we quickly were cutting past furrowed land, slouching meadows and copses of old elms and oaks. Above the flatlands outside Manningtree soared a falcon. I watched as it sailed beneath the clouds before apocalyptically plunging towards the earth, its wings folded, disappearing before elegantly rising again with a bloodied field mouse or songbird clasped between its talons. For a long time after the falcon disappeared into the meadow's vanishing point, the sight of its stoop remained with me and inversely brought to mind an image from childhood of standing in the shadow of pheasants, grouse and partridges hooked by their beaks in the butcher's window as my mother, somewhere indoors, exchanged what little money she had for a link of sausages. The thought of the falcon's stoop resulting from a bullet rather than the sight of prey stayed with me until I alighted the train and stepped into the concourse of Norwich train station.

A gruff and silent taxi driver, who listened to the football news at an intolerable volume, took me from the station to Margaret's house in Wendling, a remote hamlet surrounded by meads and dense woodlands, roughly midmost from Norwich and the nearest coast. Once I met Margaret, this positioning seemed entirely intentional as she was somebody whose skittish mannerisms and rough-hewn appearance belied her metropolitan affect and interests. Her house was set back from the main road by a short and pockmarked driveway and concealed by an overgrown thicket of blackthorn and a large mulberry tree. It took the taxi driver and me several minutes to find the driveway, and while he parked on the roadside and smoked I tried to call Margaret. With his arms resting through his window, he lamented the commentary on Norwich FC, who had just conceded a penalty to Hull City. So as not to hear the outcome, he turned away from his car window and walked to the other side of the road shaking his head. He quickly pointed out to me a slanted moss-covered post stuck into the earth that read 'Wendling Hall'. Together, we pulled away the branches, seeing then the driveway and vaguely through the tangle of dense shrubbery, the blurred contours of a grand stone house.

After paying the fare, I crouched beneath the branches and ambled down the derelict drive. To my left, a large garden sprawled wildly up to a hedgerow from where, through a break in the shrubbery, I saw rutted land drift out into a further field and from there into another and so on. The grounds of the property were knotted with bright purple cornflowers, foxgloves, wood anemones, poppies and yarrows. Large lolling bushes and shrubs bursting with glossy elderberries and rowans ran along the perimeter. The large stone house soon appeared more clearly from behind the drooping arm of a willow. It was clearly once a grand and stately home and rose three tall floors, bearing dozens of large single-paned windows, one of which was smashed and boarded up with cardboard and several others which were filled in with concrete. Algae dribbled from the cracked white rims of the windows onto the stone, and half of the roof tiles were of a different, lighter slate suggesting to me the roof had been damaged and improperly repaired. The grass of the garden rose to my knees and was gnarled with ferns and brambles, bracken and thistles. The far edge of the garden's grass contorted from the house into the thick and bulbous roots of ancient oak and ash trees, which extended into the dark woodland that bordered the northern edge of the grounds, while weeds and vines ran around the outer edge, creating the sense that the home and the wilderness that surrounded it were one living and co-acting being.

As I skulked towards her house, a sand-coloured songbird swooped from a nearby brook past me and darted into the darkness of a small bush. Above the brook, I noticed a rotting wooden bridge, one small enough to call to mind both then and now my grandmother's stories of fairies and water nymphs who, at the time of her telling us, inhabited the gardens of her house and the little stream that ran at the end of her property. As I walked on, the warbling of the songbird sounded and seemed to me then to be trying to mimic the swells and breaks of the brook as it slid over marbled grey pebbles and parted around wet brown twigs.

The day fell into shadows as a dense blanket of clouds covered the sun. The summer country air took on a quick and cutting chill. At once the element-weathered house felt desolate and abandoned. I pressed a tatty white buzzer that was slightly dislodged from the stone and stood waiting at the scullery door. A few moments passed before I heard the sound of leaden footfalls, and through a second-floor window emerged the face of a rakish and stony-looking woman. She raised her hand, beckoning to me and vanished again before reappearing at the front door.

Margaret was wearing a moth-eaten crimson cardigan, a paint-speckled navy calf-length skirt and black clogs. Her hair, wispy and sheet white, was unbrushed and strayed outward. Her eyes, two luminous green and yellow pools, shimmered beneath her smooth brow. Beneath them were lumpen sacks of drooping skin and an almost invisible white fuzz along her cheeks and upper lip. She wore thick-rimmed glasses that sat on the tip of her nose, and from above them she studied me with narrow-eyed suspicion. She sighed upon opening the door and after looking me up and down quipped, *Oh right, yes. I see the resemblance now.* She opened the door for me, and as I bent over to remove my shoes she waved me down from doing so barking, *I wouldn't, darling. It's more a place you wipe your feet on the way out.* She led me through a vestibule where not so much as a sliver of the floor or walls were visible; odd pairs of muddy shoes and green wellington boots were scattered across the floor and heaps of hanging coats bulged off the walls, narrowing the anteroom into a suffocating buffer between the wild, hidden world outside and the dim, cavernous space that existed within.

I'm going to have a tea; would you like one? she chirped as she lit a rolled cigarette. I politely declined and she led me into an outmoded kitchen and pointed me through to the living room. There were three large fabric sofas which were sunken in and fraying along the ridges and, like the position-ing of benches to a shrine, they were spread evenly around an old television. I sank into one and subtly surveyed the room. Neatly folded on the arms and backs of them were variously patterned woollen blankets. The floorspace, which was cloaked with a number of large overlapping patterned rugs, was also cluttered with odd bits of chipped antique furniture and tilting stacks of wooden chairs. Ill-fitting blue velvet curtains were drawn open above the large windows, beneath which were dozens of rolls of studio paper delicately balanced against a number of half-filled boxes and framed photographs that faced the interior walls. Like a tracker spotting the still-warm prints of prey in the snow, I sensed neglect in the swipes of dust around the edges of the curtains. It showed to me that, for the first time in years, they'd been heaved open to let the light in. Several of the boxes along the wall were filled with old family ornaments: brass statues, sepia-washed photographs of suited men, fine china, dusty crystal glasses and antique paintings. The walls of the room were covered with framed family photographs and black-and-white portraits of young men in uniform. The shelves were also bedecked with a number of intricately painted wooden statues of elephants, tigers and giraffes. Hidden in the corners, near the large curtains, I noticed several taller marble sculptures of Oriental mythic creatures. On a large bookshelf lined with leather-bound antique books – the titles of which were written in gold leaf and barely legible – was a small silver jewellery box from which emerged a ballerina and behind this, almost invisible, a picture of four people: Margaret, Max and my father as their younger selves beside an older woman I didn't recognize.

As I sat waiting for Margaret – who from the adjoining kitchen could be heard humming and preparing tea – the wide-open doors of her home and the warmth of the gusting breeze through the corridors called to mind the mother of an old childhood friend. During the summers, I would often visit my friend's home, which was situated on a large farm in the Berkshire countryside. The house, a shingled grange with Gothic-arch doorways and flagstone flooring, slouched into the ground it stood on and was surrounded by acres of pastureland. The surrounding world of little streams, woodlands, two large ponds, barns and roaming fields provided sanctuary for me and my friend. And the house at night, in front of a dwindling fire and a movie, became the hollow in which we hid from the very world just hours before we'd enjoyed. I recall that the boy's father was absent and he had no siblings and during the times I was there his mother was a loose presence: opaque, quiet, spectral and yet somewhere close at all times.

Throughout the school year, my mother would save money for my trips to the house, as without a car she would have to send me in a taxi to the farm where I would stay for weeks on end. Without having to spend too much, I'd find myself endlessly occupied and happily so too. I'd squander those days – the fabric of which now feels so tenuous and fine – clambering along the mossy boughs of sycamores and elms in the nearby woods, or sneaking into the neighbouring farm and joining my friend in hurling stones at baffled cows from a bush, enticing them to charge at us once we jumped out and ran.

Usually, after our hours of play, with my eyes swollen from pollen and my hair shooting blades of grass, I'd enter the home alone to fetch a jug of water and sweet snacks. There, I'd often find the mother of my friend sat alone at the dining table, smoking a cigarette with her eyes closed, as she blankly traced the spiral wood grain of her table with her spindly index finger. All the windows and doors in the house were open and so battling shafts of wind streamed through the corridors and rooms, occasionally blowing open or closing a door somewhere. I do not remember her expression so well anymore, but I can clearly remember the scent of burning tobacco commingled with a zephyr heavy with the scent of mowed grass, wildflowers and cherry blossoms. When she'd hear my approach, often from a distance when walking down the cobbled path, I'd watch as she would avert her eyes, rise and close the door to the dining room in which she sat, forcing me to walk through the aslant, blustering stone corridor and around into the kitchen. Upon occasion, she would leave a jug of water and snacks for me at the front door, so I wouldn't have to enter at all and silently this became our preferred arrangement.

One such day, I found all the doors of the house to be locked and returned to my friend empty-handed and confused as to why his mother, who I knew was home, would lock the doors on us. After explaining to him my issue he – having a fondness for mischief I haven't encountered again since – suggested I climb through the kitchen window to retrieve the goods. After clambering up the crumbling rock, using the gaps between the stone slabs as footholds, I slipped through the window and took the jug of water in my hand. As I crept to the backdoor, so not to disturb his mother, in the silence of the house I heard a soft, almost inaudible noise that derived from a room on the second floor. At first, I thought it might be the old house which seemed to always be creaking, and in the instant of my trying to discern the sound I realized what I was hearing was sobbing. I quietly exited and ran back to my friend, keeping the secret of his mother's latched sorrow buried deep within myself, so much so as to almost (but never quite) forget it.

The following summer, after dejectedly taking my mother's refusal to send me in a taxi to my friend's house as a sign of our ever-increasing poverty, she decidedly told me that my friend's mother had disappeared early in the summer and couldn't be found. My friend, according to my mother, had been sent to stay with his father in Hong Kong for the time being and I knew then that that summer would be all the different for it. When, some weeks later, I gathered the courage to ask my mother again if my friend's mother had been found and when he would return from Hong Kong, she expressed to me, in what would later become a lesson in brevity, the entire fate of their lives in so few words, *Charlie will be staying in Hong Kong from now on.* I knew immediately what this meant, or at least I believed I did, and as my body surged towards this awareness, I was reminded abruptly of the creaking house in the summer and the distant, almost inaudible sobbing emanating from that hidden room.

Over the edge of the sofa, I noticed a large box filled with an amalgam of rusting compositors' instruments: several wooden-handled bodkins (some broken), steel shooting sticks, combination tweezers, four large brass rule-curving machines whose bases were stamped with the word 'Caxton', foot-long wooden pica poles, slug cutters, circular and angular quads, miterers and two table saws. *That was all Max's stuff,* Margaret whispered, taking a seat on the opposite sofa. *In fact, it was his mum, Sarah's, first, if I'm not mistaken. She gave it to him when he was younger. When he died most of his things came here. He didn't want his father to have any of it, only me. That was what he requested. In his will that is. All Max's, that. Sarah's first.*

She spoke in sharp, precise sentences and with a knowing contentment and slowness that can be felt in those who harbour the information being sought. But Margaret maintained a quietness about her too, a subtle remove. Without succumbing to the pride her knowingness encouraged, I sensed the frankness and candour that comes too with exhaustion and forcibly having to make displaced acquaintance with one's past. She held only to the wish to speak of the old things in the cleanest terms possible (despite being unable to do so), all so not to disturb the black waters within herself, those which until then had taken so long to fall still.

She carried herself in a conventional fashion: sat almost entirely unmoving. Her posture was perfect and firm and she kept her knees steadily pressed together – a classroom manner residual of a bygone time. And even appearing wildly, covered in lashings of paint, I recall her roughly shooing off any floating dust or specks of lint she spotted before they had a chance to settle on her. For the first few moments of our encounter her eyes, mottled with green and yellow and magnified by her glasses, remained fixed on me. We held this mutual consideration for some time before she eventually asked, *What is it you'd like to know?*

Outdoors, it had begun to pass into afternoon, and without any lights the house allowed the shadows of passing clouds to inhabit it. After too long in silence, for a reason I am still unsure of, perhaps out of the unease I felt, I began to speak about Max's funeral. I spoke to her in a shameful unravelling of anxiety and guilt about the awkwardness I felt being there as a boy, the uncertainty of my emotions and the blankness with which I composed myself that day. Beneath it, I was trying to express to her that I didn't know Max at all and had no memory of him whatsoever, but I knew he was a man who, with immovable adoration, my late father thought of at least daily.

Once I stopped talking, once my blood cooled and all I could hear was the ticking of a hidden clock and the thudding of my heart, I sank back into the couch having caught myself crooked forward, and only then, slowly and quietly, did Margaret begin: *I long found it strange that Max died in the same town he was born. Not that it's uncommon by any measure for this to happen but with him I found it unnatural. Folkestone was a place he derided throughout his life and complained relentlessly about, even when he was miles and years from it.*

He was brought up there in a dingy terraced house with two front-facing windows and two back-facing windows that looked out onto a titchy and overgrown garden. I was Sarah's friend from childhood. We grew up together in South London and were bound to each other from the moment I caught her stuffing paintbrushes and paints into her school blazer in art class. As a child, she was troublesome and testing. The two of us together would often land each other in trouble with our teachers and our parents. Where she taught me to steal, I taught her to smoke; where she taught me about sex, I taught her about drinking. I've always felt us meeting was the colliding of two chaotic particles. At least when we were young.

Sarah met Adam at one of those godawful dances in a community hall. She was just seventeen and he was twenty-three. He had travelled up with two work friends from Kent, which was where he landed from Poland right at the start of the war with his only remaining family, his older sister, Yula, who if I remember correctly returned to Europe rather soon after the end of the war. I never knew what it was that Sarah saw in the man; I found him to be utterly repulsive and rather suspicious. He had a flat and crooked nose that almost touched his top lip, a protruding brow and dark features and rubbery lips which were purpled from smoking. At the time, he was working at Silver Spring's factory on the bottling line. Because of his job, after they married and she had Max, Sarah was forced into living in Folkestone – an idea I laughed at when I first heard. Why? Well, to pair Sarah with Kent, to me, was to place a roaring fire in an airless room. But there they went.

During the summers, Margaret explained, *I'd take the train down to visit them. In the thick of it, it gets very busy in Folkestone. It fills up with families, all there for the beach – Sunny Sands. Whenever I'd visit, Max would drag Sarah and me there. He'd beg us to go. It's a funny little beach, a typical English beach in many ways, albeit without shingle. We'd usually arrive terribly late and be left without any space on the sand, so we'd have to make do on the edge or by the harbour arm. Sarah and I would pitch up two chairs and let Max loose. He'd run himself ragged in all directions: barrelling into the water, scaling the harbour wall, but I remember, under no circumstances, did he ever go near the arches there.*

Later, when researching Sunny Sands I found there to be these rather striking concrete arches. They're set back from the beach and extend the entire length of it. On top of them is a promenade which people walk on to look out to the sea. I found something about those unnatural recesses bored into the earth to be consequential and grave; strained and yet, to some extent, bodily, like a team of engineers had pulled back the earth to reveal the structure of its bone. The pictures I found, which were largely taken from the harbour arm, showed the beach extending out from a ragged and shifting slope strewn with rough and climbing grass. And threaded between the cliff and beach were those great grey arches which look so brutish and alien, like the forgotten part of an abandoned trainline or a defensive relic of the war. When I showed the pictures to a friend, she said that the arches looked to her like the binder rings of a notebook. Her conception of them appearing as the collapsible axis of concealment between the sea and the land, a point of closure that has remained with me since.

As a little boy, Margaret continued, *Max refused to play with the other children and they with him. So, when he grew bored of swimming and playing alone in the sand, he'd ask me and his mother to go and sit on the harbour arm with him. He'd sit down in what he called 'my chair', which was this one particular spot on the edge of the wall on which the stone was eroded inward and smoothed, forming a seat. And with his bare little legs dangling over the sea below, he'd very carefully draw the arches over and over again in a sketch pad I bought for him.*

Margaret described how Max would never draw the beach or the children, or the adults swimming and sunbathing. Only, instead, would he very precisely create a totally lifeless scene that displayed only the arches and their shadows.

I would ask him, she continued with a lissom smirk, *'Why don't you try a seagull, or a tree, or a little boy named Max?' but he refused. He simply kept drawing the arches and he'd do it until he'd run out of space on his pages. It was obsessive. He'd fill all of his sketchbooks with these little drawings and then wouldn't show them to any of us. He'd keep them all to himself. He was always a very quiet and lonely boy, I thought. And as much as she tried, Sarah couldn't help much with that. It was simply the way he was. When he was little, his father and he were close. When Adam did get time off work, he'd spend all of it with Max. He'd take him into the town or down to the beach, or on long walks around Folkestone. You wouldn't believe how long he'd make the poor child walk. Sometimes, they'd set off in the morning and be gone until late at night, which would worry Sarah to death. On more than one occasion, she'd call me up in the middle of the* night in hysterics, screaming, 'Adam's taken him. They're gone!' and I'd have to calmly assure her that he'd come back safely with Max, and eventually, always he would. They'd usually arrive home at around midnight and Sarah would be in a rage. She told me that Adam would never say where they went but there was one night that Sarah questioned Max alone and he admitted to her that they had gone to the arches.

Here, I recall Margaret's rigid visage slightly loosened. Her lips, tightly pursed, fell open and some immemorial shock shuddered in her but she couldn't allow for so much as a passing pause. Firm again, she went on: *Just after Max's tenth birthday, the family moved to London. Adam found himself a job working in a garage there and moved the family into a small council apartment south of the river. I helped the family pack up their belongings into their car and mine. I drove Max while Sarah went with Adam. Max sat in the passenger side, staring quietly out the window. He was neither excited nor relieved but baffled and unable to say anything to me. Even when I asked him about his new school, or his new home, he was unable to find the words. The only person who got him to ever talk was your dad. When Max and he met at school, Max became a different person. Your father was a few years older than him but the two of them would spend all day together at school. And your dad would walk Max back to the flat with a group of other boys. Mind, your dad got Max in quite a bit of trouble at school. I remember having to go with Sarah to the school to pick up Max after he threw a paper plane from a window and it hit a girl in the eye. In the car, he shouted, 'He dared me!' talking about your dad.*

*Not long after they arrived in London, Sarah became preg-
nant with a second child – a boy named Patrick.* At this, again,
Margaret's resolute tone faltered and her gaze dropped to the
floor in front of her feet. *Patrick. He had these great blond
curls that fell about his ears, big rosy cheeks and blue eyes that
were so pale at times they looked white or even grey. He was born
prematurely, I think at thirty-three or thirty-four weeks, and so,
sadly, he struggled with learning difficulties and health problems
throughout his life. Adam could be very severe with Patrick.
Mostly out of irritation at the boy's general state of confusion. I
remember one day, Sarah called to tell me Adam had hit Patrick
over dinner, and in the background, I could hear the poor boy
wailing and Adam swearing loudly at him. And all of this happened in front of Max, and from then on he made a point to
take it upon himself to shield his younger brother from his father.
He was sensitive like that. Max would play with Patrick and
read to him at night, unlike Adam who had no patience for his
second son.*

Margaret explained that not long after Patrick was born,
Sarah met a man who lived in Brixton Hill called Leighton.
He was from Trinidad and ran a small political magazine
called *The Horizon*.

Sarah, Margaret said, *mostly helped Leighton with the ad-
ministrative tasks at the magazine, and she only did it when the
boys were at school and Adam was working. She made sure of
that much. She did it at first to make some extra cash, although
she was earning next to nothing there. Sarah had always been
interested in art and was especially good at calligraphy. She had*

a truly beautiful eye for it. Growing up, I remember she would write to us, her friends, little notes with these great swooping and diving letters. I sadly lost all of mine years ago but I can still remember how she'd do it: she'd come up to you, or a friend of hers, and put her hand to her mouth like she were going to whisper something to you and so you'd draw close to her and with her other hand, she'd slip one of those beautiful notes into your pocket without you noticing. When she hadn't said anything, you'd look up to her confusedly and she'd just giggle and then later you'd find one of those notes often just spelling your name. When she met Leighton, all that time afterwards, she had taken an interest in typography and letter-pressing and spent her free time sketching different fonts. And one day, when working in the office at The Horizon, *she told Leighton this, and he, just like that! trusted her to help them with their cover designs and formatting.*

Suddenly, Margaret stood up and rushed towards the windows. She rummaged through a box and carefully, with the dexterity of an art handler, took out a sheet of paper and brought it over to me. It was the laminated front page of an edition of *The Horizon: This was the first edition that Sarah helped design. She redesigned the font for them, and they used it until the magazine fell apart in the late 1980s. She was proud of her involvement with* The Horizon *and carefully preserved all the issues of it. Take a look, they're all in the boxes scattered around. It's all ended up with me.*

The front page of the magazine was dated 'August/September 1974', and the headline read 'Imperial Typewriters:

Strike'. Ostensibly, *The Horizon* covered topics relating to racial issues, Marxism and anti-colonialism and was run by a number of Black intellectuals, writers and artists. It also included short stories, poems and works of visual art.

Of course, Margaret continued, *Adam became irritated that Sarah was working alongside Leighton. He was very suspicious of him, I don't know why, he was suspicious of everyone. Even me! Whenever Sarah mentioned Leighton, a mad jealously came over him and he'd storm out of the room in a huff and sulk for hours like a child. His jealousy was so much that he wouldn't let Leighton come to the flat, or even let Sarah stay at the magazine's office beyond 6 p.m. One night, I remember Sarah called me to say that Adam had banned her from seeing Leighton and that he'd gone as far as showing up at the office threatening him. That was almost it for Sarah. She threatened to take the boys and leave Adam on the spot and, eventually, he did apologize and let her keep working there. That was the beginning of the end.*

During this time, Margaret explained Max began helping his mother at the magazine and had taken a discerning interest in the work she was doing. The two of them would spend hours together in the office, and Max would diligently help her with any typographic tasks and would even spend some time designing his own fonts alongside Leighton, who had become something of a mentor to Max.

Even at that age, he had a real talent for it, Margaret told me. *Just like his mother he was naturally gifted. Not only was he interested in the drawing of the fonts but he was fascinated by the mechanics of letter-pressing. He was like that, even as a boy,*

very inventive. I always thought he should've been an engineer.
She recalled to me that at the start of 1978, during a particularly bitter winter when few people could find the money to
heat their homes, Sarah, to combat the fatigue that the cold
and poverty brought with it, found two old and out-of-use
Ludlow Typographs. Max and Leighton spent two months
working together to restore them; one was for the magazine
and the other for Sarah and Max to use at home.

I was distant in those years, Margaret trembled, *but at the
time, my career was fast moving and I was setting up shows
in Antwerp, Oslo and Lisbon and rarely in London. I saw the
Mitnicks much less but I spoke to Sarah on the phone nearly
every day.* Margaret put her finger to her lips, *Perhaps, this was
never enough, for either of us. I was happy with Sarah telling
me, 'It's all fine here,' and I never pushed her on that maybe as I
should've. Perhaps, it wasn't enough. For either of us.*

Without admitting too much, Margaret was trying to
express to me both that words are never enough to understand the entirety of a thing: pieces are left out or forgotten
and the weight and intensity of the reality pales under the
infirmity of words. Words are often not enough for the
speaker either; not only as a tool of expression but also as a
means of making sense of the object of expression. In speaking, the insensible is often rendered into further insensibility
and the chaotic is given only a brief form that ultimately
remains incomprehensible.

She went on, trying: *Some weeks, Max would send me pack-
ages filled with the work the two of them did for* The Horizon,

*and briefly he became very invested in the politics of the maga-
zine and rather militant about it too. It was quite ridiculous
really. He dressed in a black beret and wore a button-down
leather jacket whose lapels were covered with garish political
pins. He looked like a total prat,* she smiled. *But like Sarah, he
was very prideful about the work the magazine did. He felt there
was something larger than him in his life, something to stand on
the side of, and I think for him that was invaluable. But still,* she
stopped to consider, *at the same time, he was growing older and
without any hope of going to university and without a well-paid
job, I suppose he was also very lost.*

In that period, Sarah and Adam bought a unit in a brick
warehouse in Stockwell with the hope of turning it into a
larger family home. They used the pennies they had scraped
together as well as most of Sarah's inheritance to do so and
kept their council apartment as they slowly renovated the
new property: *It had been a storeroom for a mechanic before,*
Margaret grinned. *It was a large dirty space filled with old
machinery, equipment and rats. It was in desperate need of
work. But I ought to say, Adam did fix it up with his own hands.
I remember, he was absolutely adamant that he wanted each of
his sons to have their own room.*

I thought, Margaret said straightening herself, *he wanted
that so badly because of his strange desire to give the life at hand
that which was different from his past. The only trouble with
this was that Adam's attempts to do so always came with a total
reluctance to ever speak about his childhood to anyone, even
Sarah. I think he hoped he would forget it by doing this.*

Margaret saying this confirmed what I had heard from my father years before: Max's mother, Sarah, was from Derry and his father, Adam, was of Polish-Jewish descent. When Adam was a child, he and his older sister emigrated to England at the start of the war and arrived in Kent. The rest of his family were lost to the camps. This experience, undoubtedly, seared an indelible and unresolved grief upon Adam that over the course of his life festered and split into an ever-deepening wound which was frequently neglected and omitted from the surface of his consciousness. The consequence of this dereliction – as Margaret and my father both theorized to me but using different words – was that there was always the quietly steaming away, latent and invisible truth of memory which sat waiting, predacious and shadowing each thought and action with an irrevocable melancholy. And upon occasion, without warning, it would seize him by the neck again to reveal itself in fits of anger and violence, long periods of absence and frenzied paranoia.

It took Adam, Margaret went on, *two years to make the home liveable, and by then Max had begun his long slide towards, well, you know . . . He would stay out for days and nights without any contact with his parents. He was very silent with his family but reckless and loud with his friends, like your father, who none of us thought was a good influence on Max, because he held these big parties all over town, and Max followed him to them all. He was already a terribly shy boy but somehow, in those years, he withdrew further into himself and away from us all. His personality was split, he would either spend his time drinking himself senseless, or in his bedroom alone quietly drawing. At some point, I don't know when exactly, he stopped working at* The Horizon. *Leighton was concerned that he'd stopped and would go over to the flat to check on him. You can only imagine how this angered Adam. The two men would end up in shouting matches – Adam peering out of the window shouting abuse at Leighton and Leighton down on the street shouting back at him. There was one night in the early 1980s, when Leighton was walking home from a talk he'd given. A group of white men followed and brutally attacked him and left him lying in the street. It was a savage and racist attack and was in the news for just a second. They shattered both his wrists, broke one of his collarbones, staved in his head with a club and broke four of his ribs. They almost killed him. And from that point on, Leighton stopped talking to Sarah and stopped talking to Max. He swore it was Adam who had been behind it. The police did nothing to help him. We never found out who did it.*

When I asked Margaret if it was Adam who had done it, she wavered: her eyes latched onto mine for a moment then fell onto the same space in front of her feet. I felt she was doubting her own suspicions and seemingly doubting my capacity to absorb them. Her eyes sailed between the box of Max's tools and an old cigarette burn in a rug on the floor. She stuttered, trying to find the correct expression, before finally saying, *He said he didn't. Swore to us. And no one knows, really.* After a further moment's pause, with her breath held and lips tightly pursed again, she opened her mouth to speak but no words emerged.

After seconds in silence, she continued: *Patrick was still unable to talk and his health was worsening. Sarah and Adam were forced to put him into a home in Nottingham to help with his needs. Whenever he'd get a cold, it'd be such a panic because he had a terribly weak immune system. I'd visit him some weekends with Sarah. I remember he was happiest in the summer playing in the fields and saddest when it was grey. He hated strong winds, when it rattles the windows or hisses under the doors. He didn't mind the rain and he'd jump up and down when it snowed. As his friends all grew up around him, Max decided to go travelling by himself in Asia. Using what he'd saved up and what little his parents gave him, he left London and stayed with the uncle of a friend of his – a man named Arman in Krabi, South Thailand.*

Margaret, again, rose and opened a chest of drawers beside the TV from which she took out a stack of four thread-bound navy notebooks. She leafed through the pages of them and closed the drawer. She handed one of them over to me and kept the remaining three in her lap, *This is what he kept from his travels.* The notebooks' covers were worn smooth in places, the binding thread was loose and fraying. Taking one of them in my hand, revolving it in my palm, I became acutely aware not only of the passage of time, but of the mute journey of the notebook itself: through the jungles and coasts of South East Asia and back to England. Accompanying Max along on his shifting journey between different apartments, houses, rooms and walls, and it being remembered, kept safe and preserved by him, despite his mutable and chaotic state.

As I held it for the first time, I recall almost dropping it, for at once coming to this realization I simultaneously felt the entire weight of Max's concentration, attention and devotion to the notebook, as it seemed to absorb the density of all those years. Each passing day, every fleeting moment and each whim of feeling all condensed into an unyielding mass that I found nauseating and unbearable to begin so much as to comprehend.

I opened it and began reading:

25 August 1982

Days here are quiet and wet. Morning rain cracks on the roof. Woken twice now by howling animals. I imagined monkeys and birds arguing in the trees. Arman tells me it is big cats fighting. With a smile. Beneath my bed I hear scratching. When I check, it stops.

Out from the house, just beyond the edge of the garden, the sea. Early morning, a mist. From behind, the sun breaks through. I sit there and watch. Sometimes sat in the rain. At the desk here. Drawing. Old things are returning.

31 August 1982

The heat at night is stifling. The air buzzes. Insects. Birds. Arman says he'll fix my fan soon but I'm not sure. He said the same a few days ago. We drove down to a river yesterday and fished. Arman sat and spoke to the locals. One old man was preparing to cremate his son who had died some days ago in a storm. They will scatter him in that river. Arman says he will go to pay his respects. I may join.

Called home. Summer almost gone there. Mum says Patrick is enjoying school. He likes to lie in the grass and watch the sky. I can see him. Smiles all day long. I can see him, even here. Happy days.

2 September 1982

Day of the fisherman's funeral. I asked Arman if I could go with him. He dressed me in ceremonial clothes. For the first time in a long while it didn't rain. Flickering sun. Light breeze. We stayed at the river till evening. Candles lit. Seemed hundreds of people went.

By night, the glow of fires on the black river. Total darkness other than the reflection of the candlelight. If I focused for too long on it, it felt I was looking out into something. The night sky. If I believed it, I saw it. Only the ashes on the surface, sinking into the depths, broke the illusion. There, with the prayers of the ceremony. The silence. The chanting. I felt there were spirits among us. An otherworldly force surrounding us. I began to cry. The darkness brings about strange things in me. It's unbearable at times.

Bad dreams. Pool of my own sweat. I was sure someone was in my room. I couldn't see. I felt a presence. There was no one there. I dreamt someone had broken into my room. It wasn't a figure but a shadow of some kind. The fear didn't go away.

4 September 1982

Early morning, I took Arman's car out for a drive along the coast. The geography of this country is immersive in every sense: dense, sprawling jungles, the presence of life, invisible too.

Noon. Stretching out into the sea, I noticed a wooden pier with crowded shanty houses built on top. The beach around shingled with smooth stones, plastics, metals and driftwood. The houses supported by spindly stilts. Beneath, squatting children and adults sifted through the waste, drifting in the shadows. The arches back home. As I stepped closer, the crouched people all stopped and looked at me. They became absolutely still. Their silhouettes like apparitions. Like the stuff of children's nightmares. I left.

I drove into the jungle. I took a dirt road up a small mountain that Arman had circled on a map. I wound beneath the swooping and knotted vines, the jumping and suspicious animals. The colourful birds cawing. On the forest floor, splintered banyan trees netted together. Elder tualang trees pushed through the canopy. The thousand-year tree roots ruptured the dirt, covering the forest floor in dark knots.

I brushed my hand along the trunks and imagined those moments of growth, of unseen motion that existed all around me. That still moved. The sight of oneself was like beholding a single grain of sand dissolving on a seabed.

As when I sat on the riverbank, overcome by the grandeur of the earth, its dark lands and black depths. I felt then the quiet and coordinated movement of time's hand. Warm rains poured and I remained and soaked a little before sitting in the car, dozing to the sound of rain shattering against the windows. When it stopped, a new silence. The sun pierced the cloud cover, releasing pressure and washing the jungle and the earth in a faint light.

I waited until sunset on the edge of the forest, towards the top of the mountain. As night fell, I drove back down the path and homeward. I couldn't escape the sense that this jungle, the forest, the mountain represented all of nature and that this hidden world was in some way nature herself. To leave would be to abandon it.

5 September 1982

Arman cooked rice and boiled vegetables. We ate together under the awning. I told him about my drive up the mountain and into the jungle. He called my feeling 'transubstantiation'. He did try to explain it. I tell him about my dream. About my fear that there was someone in my room the other night. He laughed. Thinking of Patrick tonight.

Black of night. Sure again someone was in my room. Their shadow stood in the frame of my door. Lights on. Nothing. Bad dream. Same dream. I tried to sleep the rest of the night with my light on. Failed. I wandered out into the garden to watch the sunrise. Slept out there till daybreak.

7 September 1982

Arman takes me back to the mountain. We leave the car close to where I listened to the rain. He walks me down through the forest. Moist and alive. The canopy conceals the sky. Despite it being early morning, it felt like night. We find a grassy flat. Roots and plants grow between. Camouflaged insects shift across the surface. Arman tells me these are the ruins of an old Buddhist temple. They built it here in the forest because they believed that at daybreak and twilight spirits appeared and roamed the area. Arman chanted at the temple. We walked to the viewpoint and sat. I drew the horizon. He read. We enjoy the moments of silence between us. I feel we understand that much of each other.

For dinner he cooked pork noodles. We stayed up late drinking white cans of beer. Drunk, he told me that his late girlfriend had died in a road collision ten years ago. I sensed nothing in him. No feeling. Not for lack of it, he just seemed tired by the thought. I showed him my drawings. We slept.

Woke to screaming coming from the main house. Ran inside. Arman upright on the sofa, weeping. He couldn't catch his breath or stop crying. Eventually, he calmed. He kept saying, 'Sorry.' He had dreamt about his partner and her crash. He told me he didn't ever talk about it. I took him to his room. I left him to sleep.

9 September 1982

No sign of Arman all day. Car gone and house empty. I called home today. Patrick has fallen sick and Mum needs me home sooner. I will leave on the 12th now.

Arman returned at 2 a.m. Silently. No cries from the house tonight. Trying to sleep, lying in the darkness. Lots of thoughts swirled in me. I began to pack.

Woke from a bad dream. Same one. A presence there in my room: unwelcome and stronger than me. This time, it followed. I wasn't in my room. I was by the sea. It seemed under the pier of the shanty houses. Under something. It wasn't a wasteland, but stretching sands. Just myself in these shadows.

10 September 1982

Arman up early and smiling. He prepares fresh fruits and coffee. We sit under the awning. I tell him I am leaving sooner now. He apologizes again to me for the other night. He continues to do so even after I explain Patrick is sick in hospital with a fever. He promises to drive me back to the mountain one last time tomorrow. He pleads with me to stay. I tell him I'll still pay him the full price. He stops.

At noon, I took the car down to the beach again. I went looking for the pier of shanty houses but couldn't find my way back to it. I drove for hours along the water looking but there was nothing. I stopped for a while between two resorts and sat on the wall facing the sea. The sky, stormy and low. In the shallows, I noticed a number of wooden stumps surfacing and submerging. I thought the pier might have been destroyed by the sea. By the winds. By a storm. As I walked through the shingle, avoiding the glass, plastic and waste, an old man with a long stick balanced across his back draped with cheap sunglasses and necklaces approached me. It was the man who had scattered his son's ashes into the river. He recognized me and we spoke briefly. I asked him about the shanty houses in the sea and he told me it was further north from there. I told him I was leaving Arman's soon. He nodded and continued walking.

I drove north. Dusk falling. On the horizon, the lights of boats. The sea, hidden by evening, was just a widening void between me and the fishermen. The light of the moon and the car eventually lit up the pier. I parked. It was too dark to draw the structure. Tomorrow, perhaps. It was black out. I walked to the water's edge, beside the stilts. As I stood there, I heard footsteps from beneath the decking on the shingle. There were two figures. I became anxious and moved into the moonlight and a man appeared with a young boy beside him. The man looked at me. The young boy hung his head, avoiding me and seemed tearful. They remained in silence and walked onto the beach and around up onto the decking. I heard their door close above me.

Unable to sleep for more than an hour. Tonight: no shapeless presence just hollowness. I can't escape the little boy's face.

11 September 1982

Early morning. Sat on the garden's edge watching the mist on the sea. The world is still, like its rotation has stopped and the slow plodding of unconscious life is in the thick drifts of cloud stuck in the sky. It's like I am the only one awake in the world. I lie back in the grass and wait for Arman to come with coffee.

Mango and dragon fruit under the awning. Few words. Heavy rain on the drive up to the mountain forces us to pull over and wait. Roadside trenches flood. The stench of dead plants hangs in the air. I crack the window to take in the sound of the rain against the tarmac, the car, the jungle, the mud. It is crackling and foaming, bubbling and fuming. A strange sense overcomes me when I close my eyes to listen. The sense of the world and I being engulfed in flames.

Rain stops. Arman takes us to a different part of the mountain. The other side that looks inland. We find a narrow, concrete path cracked by underlying roots and follow it down a slope. As we walk the path disappears beneath us. Our bodies become compressed under the tangled, hanging vines and branches. We eventually emerge through the thickest part of the jungle and appear on the side of a slope.

Looking down, we see a rice field. A handful of workers. Arman moved down the slope. I disappeared back into the darkness of the forest. I became lost and wandered until I found the concrete path. I followed it until I saw off to my right a small opening in a thicket. There was a sharp relief in the earth where it was and so I entered through it to find in the clearing a blue pond. The water was stunningly clear, so clear that fallen trees and bits of dead plant matter appeared naked on the pond's grey floor and through the water glided large, slender fish. On the other side of the pond, not ten metres from where I was stood, was a straw fishing hut. The roof, a curved, arching shape was supported by sturdy branches, hacked and fashioned into stilts. The dried palm-leaf roof created a darkness within. I walked around the perimeter of the pond towards the structure and stood there for a moment. It was only when I sat down on the edge of the hut, allowing my feet to dangle in the water, did I turn and notice a body lying inside. Startled, I edged away. The man, who had been sleeping on a mat, woke and emerged from the shade. His face was puffy. His white shirt doused in sweat. He felt familiar. I apologized to him and he responded in Thai. He sat on the decking with his legs crossed and stared at me. He firmly picked the sleep from his eye, coughed and lit a cigarette. He passed one to me too. He watched the water closely and pointed at a thin black fish passing beneath the decking, speaking in Thai as he did. He stood and stripped, the sun glistened off the beads of sweat along his chest and back. His skin was marked with throbbing welts. He didn't hide his penis from me, which was nestled within a bush of black pubic hair, nor show any shame. In fact, he stood there for a moment in the sun, entirely nude and watched me as I looked back at him. He waited a moment, smiled, then dived into the water. His complexion became whitish. He swam to the other edge of the pond, disappearing from my sight and remained underwater for one maybe two minutes. Eventually, he resurfaced on the other side into a beam of sunlight. He was holding two slender and oily black fish which struggled in his grip. He tightened it around them and smashed their heads on a nearby rock, stilling them. He appeared to me then as both full of air, lacking earthly presence and at the same time, heavy and unquestionably of this world. He squatted on the other shore and began to cut and skin the fish with a thin and sharp rock. I quickly realized the familiarity I had felt. It was the man who had appeared from under the pier the other night with the little boy beside him. I suddenly felt nauseous and a sail of fear drew out in me. I felt my breath quicken and a sweat break. As he wrapped the diced fish meat in a large green leaf, he turned to me with blank and lifeless eyes and dived back into the water towards me, holding the parcel of fish above the surface. I rose off the fishing platform and ran back towards the slope on the other side to the relief in the earth until I found the concrete path. I managed my way back to the car where Arman was waiting and we drove back down the mountainside with the windows open. The setting sun. The dying light. This time, the sense of awe I felt when I first visited the mountain had disappeared. I felt a pang of fear, of danger. We wound down through the great trees that seemed now to envelop us in shadows. This feeling only subsided as we pulled out onto the road home and away from the jungle.

Arman prepared steamed dumplings for us. We ate and sat on the edge of the garden until twilight. He spoke mostly about tomorrow's travel. I said few words. An early night. Home tomorrow. Dreamless night.

The written diary entries ended there. The remaining pages of the slender notebook were filled with drawings. Meticulously drawn beneath the last entry was a detailed sketch of the concrete arches at Sunny Sands. No life, no people, only the blackness and shadows within the arches. The other drawings, poorer and hastily sketched, seemed to be of the pier he had written about, and as well of the candlelight on the water at the funeral. Max had planned to spend two months travelling but due to Patrick's illness and an unmentioned struggle with his finances, he returned home earlier than he planned.

Within only a few weeks of him returning, Margaret said limply, *Patrick passed away from meningitis. Sarah suffered terribly after that. As did Max. While she stayed in the apartment, Max moved into the house in Stockwell. I returned to London around then and spent most of my time with Sarah as she grieved. When I think back, I see it was Max who was neglected here. He would disappear for nights on end, often with your dad, and after several violent rows with his father, he left the house. Sometimes, he'd stay with his mother in her apartment but she often depressed him more. I suppose this was because,* Margaret quaked, grasping for thought, *in facing her pain, he was forced to face his own. And it was a pain I believe he would've preferred to forget. That was the way he was. But he couldn't. He stayed with your dad for some time at his place in Stockwell. And he took a job as a cleaner at St Mary's Hospital. He hated that job like you wouldn't believe and was eventually able to move to the mail room which he enjoyed more. I suppose the work was less intensive, less physical. He was awfully lazy, that's for certain. But the lulls in the postal job were better for him, only because he was able to draw. I was told, but am not sure if it's true, that in this time he attempted to get in touch with Leighton again but his efforts were met with silence. You can hardly blame the man for that.*

Margaret then detailed to me the mechanisms by which Max was able to eventually get his own council flat in Acton. And how a close friend, after years of trying to help him, fixed him a job as an office clerk at the Baltic Exchange.

When Max heard he got the job, he immediately called me to ask if I could help him pick out a suit from Marks & Spencer with his mum. He was anxious and didn't know the first thing about formal dressing, so the whole trip was chaos, she smiled. *He was picking out dark purple suits, tuxedos and floral ties. It was like watching a child attempt to dress like an adult. We had to teach him then, at the age of twenty-eight, how to tie a tie, how to polish his shoes and how to press a shirt. He was hopeless. He kept repeating, 'I need to make a good impression tomorrow,' then he'd laugh nervously with this shrill cackle.*

Afterwards, I took them both out for lunch and we walked around Wormwood Scrubs until twilight fell. I remember Sarah was beaming. She couldn't stop smiling. I remember watching as the exhaustion that consumed her face – the deep lines etched into her forehead, her ever sleepy and worried eyes – seemed to disappear entirely, even if it was just for that day. And I remember realizing that this was the first time I'd seen her even slightly happy in years. And I remember thinking, 'If only it would last. If only it would last,' and with that came the feeling in me, as pure and intractable as I've ever felt it, that it wouldn't. That it couldn't. I remember those two feelings well; I felt them both so deeply in me, in my stomach, in my chest, in my mind. I wanted it to last for her. There was no way it could.

In a brief pause, Margaret inhaled and her tone flattened again: *I left them alone there in Wormwood Scrubs. And for some reason, I can't forget the sight of them as I went: arm in arm, laughing as they vanished into the evening, homeward.*

She sunk into silence and wiped a tear from her eye that hadn't yet appeared. Her hand rifled around in her handbag, which was slumped beside her on the floor, and snapped out an old picture of Max in his odd-fitting suit beside a beaming lady who she told me was Sarah and who I recognized as the older lady from the picture of her, Margaret, Max and my father. She handed me the picture and as I studied the photo, staring deeply into those overexposed faces, a dense mist simultaneously felt to part and appear in me. It seemed an essential truth was revealed in the photo, endlessly glittering and darkening like mica in the dim hill's granite. What that truth was ineffable and formed incompletely in me, like whispered descriptions of the natural world, a familiar orison spoken in a foreign language, one's former homeland emerging through the fog from the plane window, the old song's use in recapturing the time of listening, the voices of loved ones as you sleep, the smell of lost ones on their old clothes. I couldn't say for certain what I gleaned from the photo, or rather what was spoken to me by it, only the sense of the feeling of knowing completing in me before disintegrating again.

She continued: *After the bombing at the Baltic Exchange, Max became completely frightened to go to work, or even to leave his home. He developed a terrible paranoia and would wake Sarah in the middle of the night, calling her about a van outside his house, or a neighbour who he thought was building a bomb. He stopped showing up for work and eventually lost his job. When Sarah told me the news, she didn't cry or talk with emotion of any kind. Instead she spoke very quietly, almost inaudibly but sternly and coldly like a doctor delivering a terminal prognosis. Beneath it, no matter what, I could hear the world-shattering realization that this would be Max's life: the constant to and fro, neither here nor there, between work and unemployment, stability and chaos, money and poverty – this was it for him. And she knew that. Soon after, he returned to the post room of the hospital and in his down hours, he continued to draw.*

I know that from this time, Max stayed with my parents and struggled with his health. When my parents left the country in 1992 for Boston, they handed their lease over to Max. In this time, he met a blond doctoral student of Anthropology at Royal Holloway called Patrick. The two of them began a brief but intense relationship. They had met at a small gathering at a pub, and Max, just that first night, according to Margaret, shared his drawings and typography with Patrick.

The morning after they met, Margaret grinned, Max called me up all chipper. I mean he was in a total state of frenzy. He told me the story of what had happened and was so full of joy, so excited that I had to slow him down, saying, 'Calm down now, tell me from the start,' and he would catch his breath and start again.

A smile broadened across Margaret's face then quickly puckered away. I noticed her habit of pursing her expressions into sly, quivering stillnesses. They were moved from her but dampened, so pulsed beneath her skin like swelling waves covered only by a silk veil. *Patrick, she said, did try and encourage Max to take his artwork more seriously. I believe Max even began to paint and continued to draw but now with more intent and a sense of destination.* With Margaret's words, it became clear to me that before there was no ending, no horizon, no beacon pushing through the haze he lived in. It was as if his whole field of vision was clouded by a fog that became denser, more impenetrable the longer he remained within himself. I imagined that Patrick, a partner, helped disperse it in him, even if only momentarily.

He became less private about his work, Margaret recounted. He even began to show it to me! There were drawings and paintings hung everywhere in his home; beautiful, abstract works which covered the walls. When I visited, he would talk to me about his art, explain it to me, and at the time he seemed close to something, like he was approaching a result in his work and his thinking. Rather naively, I was convinced by it all and offered to help him where I could but he refused. He insisted upon doing it himself. I firmly believed he had finally found the direction to follow. Still, whenever I'd talk to Sarah about it, she was less convinced. She was enthused by it; don't mistake me, or at least she contrived to be, but often she'd wearily say, with her worried eyes, 'It's great. For now.' Things like that. And I would protest and say silly things, childish to think about now, like, 'You must be happy! You must be!' and she'd say, 'I am. No really. I am,' then tiredly force a smile.

One night, Margaret sighed, after we met with Max and Patrick for a pub lunch, Sarah and I walked back to hers for tea, which we usually did after meeting each other. The lunch had dissolved into late afternoon and was full of laughter and old stories. Sarah remained somewhat quiet throughout the meal, laughing, smirking at things, joining in from time to time but mostly staying hush. I felt that for some reason she was somewhat mistrustful of it all. I remember thinking it must be Patrick! she must not like him, but once we got back to hers, sat on her couch and chatted for a while, she fell very still and said to me with the tremendous vulnerability and insight I so adored her for, 'My son sits on the edge of oblivion. That is his condition.' I realized then what she was mistrustful of was her child.

Margaret thought that in Max there was something that plagued him; some dormant and inescapable darkness in him that would, at times, disappear from view but was always buried within him like a fabular sleeping giant. And whether then at lunch, or perhaps she'd always been aware, Sarah saw that the wakening force could be so much as a soundless whisper, an airless breeze. Margaret admitted to me that she was never sure of the reason for Patrick and Max's relationship ending. I explained that my father said it was alcohol but my mother would often say it was violence, as though the two exist only separately.

Their relationship, Margaret said, *didn't last long and nor did their living situation. Max was quickly evicted from his house and moved back into his mother's apartment, back into the room that he and his brother, Patrick, had once shared. It was a terribly small room, unchanged from his childhood: the walls covered in the same peeling wallpaper, the same single beds, and the same ornaments and possessions, most of which belonged to Patrick. Max was thirty-two then, it had just gone 1994. Whenever I'd go and visit, he'd hardly even leave his room. He wouldn't speak a word to me anymore, and if he did it would be one word, maybe two and would always take some effort to ply from him. He'd usually come out of his room unwashed, his head bowed and sheepishly he'd wave at me. His body became very rigid and tense; he held his shoulders up by his neck and kept his head crooked always to the floor. Sarah, meanwhile, had become severely unwell. I'd known Sarah since we were children, I'd been beside her in some truly awful times and some beautiful ones too, and I could see in her she was ill. Her face was bloated and lumpy and she'd taken on this terrible pallor. Her hair thinned tremendously, and she'd also become unlike herself: mousy and childlike. I often left their apartment in tears, utterly inconsolable. I couldn't stop myself from picturing the two of them, these two withering things, sat in rooms separated only by inches of drywall, spending each day in dumb pain, waiting for something, I don't know what, and it never appeared. It brought about such agony in me that I stopped meeting Sarah in her apartment and asked that she meet me at a café or a park. At first, she did. Then she quickly stopped as she had become so self-conscious about her appearance, she had no confidence to go outside. Overnight, she found it difficult to summon the energy to leave her home, to open the door, to get up off the sofa, which she had begun to sleep on, or even to bathe. She refused to see a doctor. She was always tired and would sleep all day. She began to get terrible cluster headaches that were so severe she'd be left incapacitated for days. It wasn't long after that she began to take painkillers with codeine in them. Without me noticing at first, she became addicted and would spend her days in a haze, drifting through life from sleep to sleep, disordered by the drugs. I would visit her and always find her weak and confused in front of the television. She would speak with a swollen tongue, unable to pronounce her words properly. She'd look at me with a pale and diminishing gaze that was so light, so languid, it was clear she was struggling to remain awake.*

Unknowing how to continue, Margaret leant forward and picked up her cold tea from where she'd set it down. She took a small sip, then noticing its chill, put it back where it had been. She looked at me and shook her head. I sensed her discomfort and wanted to say something back to her but hadn't the words. After a brief silence, she spoke all she had the strength to: *The last time I saw Sarah, I cleaned her apartment. Scrubbed the kitchen. The bathroom. The living room. Mopped the floors. Hoovered. The place was filthy. There were stacks of plates of rotting food. Cups of congealed milk. A bowl of bananas bursting with flies. Max wouldn't even come out to help. He couldn't. They were living together like two invalids. When I went to sit in the living room, she was half-asleep on the sofa. Totally out of it on painkillers. She was terribly muddled. Unable to even remember who I was. She thought at first I was a cleaner and then complained to me, as she clutched her head and winced, 'My headaches are getting worse and worse.' I began to cry. I tried to lift her off the couch to see a doctor. She refused and screamed at me. Screamed at me like she never had before. Like I was evil. I was so upset I began shouting back at her. Screaming horrible things. I knew I was saying goodbye. I knew all the visits, the calls, the hours we'd spent together were small farewells, all merging to form what was now the final one.*

As it had done earlier, Margaret's gaze crashed to the floor. But this time it was not the floor ahead of me but the space that lay directly in front of her own feet, the few inches of cold stone that divided two of the patterned rugs. Her stiff, upright posture had eased into a hunch and her shoulders hunched over, as though to protect her chest and the quietly ticking heart that was caged within. Her eyes had widened into disbelief and her hands, still perfectly entwined on her lap, were shaking violently: *I can see her now as I shouted. Beyond confusion. Not understanding that my rage was not rage. I can see her now. A little child. The little girl who once slipped me beautiful notes in class. Who with me would steal art supplies. I can see her now. Hoping for a lighter, different life. I can see her now. The woman whose melancholy she couldn't escape.*

I wouldn't be near her again until I visited Kensal Green Cemetery for her funeral. Her stone now set between her two sons.

After some time frozen in that odd position, Margaret slowly sharpened upwards again like a burgeoning stalk and disappeared into another room for many minutes. I remained alone, devoid of clear thought, as in me a number of distorted fragments attempted to assemble into something linear but found themselves repeatedly unable. An immense noise eddied in me, stirring that which was dormant and concealed. As I tried to still the motion, distilling the vast, rapidly turning collage into static and individual images in order to tether together the untethered, I found my mind lapsing into the same guiltless paralysis I experienced when sat alone at the wake, watching drunken mourners weep and embrace on a dance floor, and when a photographer beckoned to me and snapped a picture with a bright flash that both momentarily and everlastingly blinded me to that which had unravelled behind me, as well as to all that lay ahead.

When Margaret returned, her steely affect had renewed in her. Harsher and more exact than even at the start, she apologized and went on: *Max came and stayed with me at my home in London before I sold it. I put him up in the spare bedroom. I was worried he would do something terrible, so I kept a close eye on him. At first, he struggled to do anything at all. He would simply lie there in a dark room and sleep all day. When he did come down to eat or shower, he was very blank, emotionless almost, and shut off from any conversation. He'd grunt a few words here and there but really nothing more than that. I had things for him to paint and draw with and even set up his old typesetter in my shed. But he never used any of it. Not once.*

Margaret took two of the remaining notebooks from beside her and passed them to me, keeping the fourth on her lap. They were the same colour, the same binding, the same wax thread as the notebook I'd read from. But the insides of these were filled with myriad drawings and strange writings. There were meticulously considered sketches of old landline telephones, sofas, metal bed frames, classic cars like an old Rover P6 (which was a model I would later find out Adam had once owned), dining chairs, bedside tables – all obsessively, over and over again. Margaret explained that many of the objects, if not all of them, had at some point been owned by the Mitnick family.

If you see the dates in the corner, she said, *he drew these immediately after Sarah's death, when he was living with me. He quite miraculously filled the notebooks with drawings of familiar objects: ones from his childhood, from his younger years in Folkestone, things that had long been disposed of. When I found them, I was amazed and I adore them more than anything* else I own. I don't know how he remembered some of the things in there, some of them from when he was just an infant. You wouldn't expect him to remember, not the detail of them, the brand names and so on, but he did and he put them all into those drawings. They're a testament to his brilliance.

He stayed with me for nine months, and over the course of that time he did become more conversational and open. He never spoke about his mother. You simply couldn't bring her up in front of him. So, I avoided the subject like the plague. Your parents and some other friends visited him several times and would take him out with them on long drives. He appreciated that. When the time came, Max tried to speak to Adam and they tried to have a relationship but there was something between them that meant it never lasted more than a few phone calls, or a few visits either way, before Max got into a fury with him. Sometimes, he would scream to me about his father, saying he was pure evil — the devil incarnate. I'd calm him down and tell him, 'But he's your father.' It never did much. He wouldn't ever listen.

One morning in winter, Max came down to breakfast and told me he'd be leaving that week. He was funny like that. I had no issue with him staying or anything. Of course not. But he explained he had applied to be a carer at a hospice down in Folkestone and had got the job. He had found a small apartment in town above a fish-and-chip shop, not far from the water. This came as a total surprise to me. I thought it was a lie. I thought he might be joking. But when he showed me the images of the apartment and the letter of acceptance, I couldn't argue with him. He asked for a little money for his deposit and his first *month's rent which, of course, I gave him, and by the end of that week he moved out. Just like that.*

I was rather sad, she admitted. *I helped him pack his belongings up and in them found an old photograph of his brother, Patrick, and Sarah cheek-to-cheek. Seeing their faces, those two ghosts, thousands of memories I had hidden from myself rose up in me and coursed through my body like a rush of blood;* as images, singular shots from which, in no more than a second, entire days, weeks and months played out in her. And each image, like part of some faltering and meandering composition, was accompanied by the sweetest feeling, and in equal measure the most aching, which when combined causes a knot somewhere between your stomach and your heart that cannot be loosened, that devours you whole, that leads you, at the end of the ever-funnelling stream of sensations, dreams, feelings, months and years, towards what is as close and as distant as you can come to of perceiving yourself, to finding your own vanishing image.

Max, she stuttered, her crabbed body now consumed by shadows, *told me not to tell Adam or anyone else about his move. He wanted to settle first. I respected that. It wasn't until your father told me that he'd hardly heard from Max in that time, having cut himself off from everyone, that I felt I should've done more to prevent that from happening. But you see, I was just trying to help him. It hurt a lot of people, including your father, who never understood why his friend had treated him so and sadly passed away not ever knowing.*

Confirming what my father had told me too, Margaret explained Adam's various illnesses which included: incapacitating arthritis, benign but excruciating skin lesions that covered his back and neck, and the pharyngeal cancer that caused him immense suffering in the final years of his life but never killed him. One of my father's few observations about the Mitnicks that he freely offered to me was his enduring belief that Adam's physical ailments were a kind of punishment handed down to him by a mystic court, which penanced him with solitude and unending illnesses. My father seemed to harbour an unwavering and at times seething anger for Adam which bared itself in random moments.

After Max left, Margaret said, *Adam would call me to ask about him. He'd ask if I had been in contact with him, if I'd seen him and how he seemed. But Max never called, never visited and never asked after his father. Long after Max's death, when Adam was dying, I would travel to help him where I could. It would usually just be to take him to the hospital, or to help him if he was having trouble with groceries and cleaning around the house. I did this until he was finally moved into a hospice. I can still see Adam, the two of us sat in his living room, like us now and him saying to me with wet eyes, 'I built this house for my family, only for me to live in it alone. I built my own prison.'*

The last time I saw Max, she dwindled, *I went down to visit him one summer. He met me at the train station. I remember him wearing a long navy trench coat and wire-frame sunglasses. He'd lost weight but had aged a lot too. His skin seemed inflamed and he looked ashen to me like he was physically fading. He told me that he had been walking lots and had plotted out an eight-mile walk along Abbott's Cliff to the old sound mirror which he completed several times a week. He took me to the fish-and-chip shop beneath his home but I didn't go up to his apartment. Instead, we walked down to a pub by the beach and talked and talked and talked. I had just sold my house in London after inheriting this crumbling home from my mother. We scratched the surface a little and I told him about Adam and his ailments but he didn't say anything. He talked to me about his work at the hospice and particularly about an old lady named Xandra, who was sharp as a tack and would discuss art and poetry with him. Totally enthused, he told me that she could recite entire passages of Yeats, Wilde and Keats, and had given him a book of Blake's drawings, which he was sad not to have seen sooner in life.*

As the sun began to set, she said, her voice once again settling into the whisper she began with, *we walked through the town and I asked that we go to Sunny Sands. We ambled along the promenade that was above the arches and stood there for some time admiring the sea. I told him about when he was a boy and how he'd play alone and ask to sit on the harbour and draw the arches that we were stood above. I laughed. He didn't. I asked if he had any of the drawings left. He said he'd thrown them all away. We stood there in silence, listening to the waves gently break. We watched the crowds clear from the beach. We watched the tide slowly sweep inward. As we turned to walk back to the station to catch my train, he went to say something to me but didn't, or couldn't. Instead he looked far into me with his still and kind eyes, which despite being brown seemed lighter then, as if they too were greying, and he smirked at me, his eyes thinned and, in his calm, I felt and heard a thunder of words where there was instead only the blowing of the leaves, the whispering of the grass and the creaking of a locked gate.*

As we approached the station, he began to talk to me about dear Sarah and told me that a night didn't pass him without a thought of her and his brother. By the end, he regretted so much. So many things. But now, despite all that, he said he felt free. He said he felt light and that the world to him felt thin, so thin that it might lift up and float off. He embraced me and saw me off from the platform. He stood watching the train pull out until I was at last out of his sight and he out of mine.

When I received the call just a few months later, I must admit, I felt relief. I went down to his apartment to clear his possessions, as at the time Adam was in hospital. He asked that I throw out all his belongings, but when I arrived there were only a few things there: his clothes, his watch on the nightstand, the picture of Sarah and him, the Marks & Spencer suit hanging in his closet, the note he left and those four notebooks.

Margaret then passed me the final notebook, which for some reason, in that moment, I felt anxious to open. When I eventually did, I found it to be filled from cover to cover with just one thing – highly detailed drawings of the arches. Over and over again, from different angles and different vantage points, in different sizes; some imagined, as if drawn from out on a boat or from a passing plane. There was nothing else on the pages: no words, no dates – only the arches. All the drawings were lifeless, airless, motionless; totally still, totally pure, as if after so long he had finally understood how to capture them, how to comprehend them in their truest yet most incomplete form while also, somehow, keeping them intact. There was a striking beauty about the monotony of them all on the page and within them all there was, I felt, a sense of ease.

As we sat there in that darkening room, an ecclesiastic silence, echoing and ringing with images, descended between us. Without disrupting it, I took out my phone and showed Margaret the picture of myself that led me to her. She took the phone in her hands and inspected it closely, zooming in a number of times and holding it close to her face. Slowly that pulsing and pursed grin appeared again. She passed me back my phone and in the sturdy manner she had earlier beckoned me with, said, *I took that picture.*

I smiled but didn't ask any further questions. As again, sat there, I felt that same sense I had felt so many years ago as a boy sitting beside my quiet father who stared down at his feet in the taxi; avoiding adults on the graveyard path, listening to their feet trudge ahead of me; bewildered, watching drunk and lifeless mourners stomp and loll across a dance floor, and of course, when a strange, slender hand upped and called my attention to it and flashed a picture of that very expression.

Without my realizing, sitting across from that woman for all those hours, I had slipped steadily into that same naive daze, which was perplexed and unknowing, and struggled to apprehend what – even after having been told the history

– remained and what was lost. I desperately combed through the words I had heard and tried to cling to each one, but all that presented itself was the void that underscored each word she spoke, like the language of the unspoken was as vast and eternal as the sayable. Sensing this, my desperation hushed in me and a beating steadiness took hold. It was an understanding that the knowable would forever remain unknowable and the sayable would forever remain pale, ghostlike, evasive.

The month after my mother at last succumbed to the illness she suffered from for so long, I left Oxford once more and found myself settling far from all I knew, for what became a protracted stretch of time in a sleepy town in Maine. I took a job there working as an archivist at a local heritage museum and spent most of my time solitarily sifting through crumbling collections of letters, articles, reports and photographs in order to log them into a digital system. The museum's archive had for years been neglected: stacks of boxes and papers, books and files had been festering in a small and fetid room on the top floor of the museum for decades, and it was my job to organize the rotting stacks of cardboard into decipherable information.

I rented a small studio space above a key-cutting shop. I paid a pittance for it and was ordered by the landlady, no matter the circumstance, to never sleep in the studio, *It's only for work*, she'd repeat to me. But of course, having no other money, I slept there every night and it became my living space. I would spend much of my week dedicating my focus so intensely upon my work that when I returned home in the evening I had no mental energy to work on what it was I hoped to work on, to complete whatever it was I'd begun.

In fact, the scrutinizing attention to minuscule details on half-faded and broken texts, all within the museum's cramped and sweltering attic space, often brought on headaches and pangs of pain so intense that when returning to my studio I needed to sit in the dark, dozing with my feet on my desk.

It was in these moments of darkness and listlessness that without provocation strange memories would surface in my mind. Odd details and flickers of conversations I'd had years before would sound so clearly it was as though those distant people were present with me then. When, in truth, all that really sounded was the creaking of boats pulling against the pier, the odd passing of a car and the distant lull of the waves breaking on the beach.

Occasionally, when I slipped into this stupor I was reminded of conversations with old friends and family, the details of many I have since forgotten. Amid them all, however, was one such story that my mind continuously fell upon for a reason I cannot be sure of. It was a story that my father (who by then was several years in the grave) told me, some months before I moved in with Sulli, on a winter's evening as we slurped bowls of hot soup in his apartment in London. The story and its telling remain to me as characteristic of him in its totality, as for some time after he passed, it was a story I found bearable to think of him through and one in which his person, his image – my memory of those at least – steadily crystalized within, even if only for an instant, like a silvery fish passing through a shaft of light in a dark and quiet pond.

In the years before I was born, when my parents were both still young and adventurous, they made several trips to Tunisia, staying at the Hôtel Club Riadh each time. And once or twice, when I was a toddler, they would leave me with my grandmother in Boston, so that they could return there together. It was in those days that I first glimpsed those three towers. My first hearing of their trips came from my mother: she would often explain her deep love of Tunisia to me as a boy, its ancient and rugged landscape, the acceptance she felt there and always from that point – after those necessary prefaces – she'd briefly outline her various stays in the country. She had been the one to ask my father to visit the country first after having read *The Tremor of Forgery* as a student. Then, at the time of reading it, her concerns had been the novel's concerns: one's sense of conflict with their native land, morally and spiritually, as well as her lifelong sense of being a stranger, an outsider, within that land.

My mother had also been fascinated by the struggle of the country and perceived it as it was: an interstice of conflict and occupation, a scarred and torn land that had taken on and shifted (doubtless, as many occupied countries do) to the forms and sways of its hosts, while retaining its essential essence. What, however, was more important to her was what lay beneath the quivering wake of its more contemporary conflicts – its rich and ancient history. She was interested in seeing the Carthage ruins at Tophet and the Roman amphitheatre, the sea-facing baths of Antoninus and the crumbling relics of Phoenician cities and cemeteries scattered up and down the coast.

Despite having been open for many years, the Hôtel Club Riadh in north-western Tunisia has not yet fallen into disrepair or a state of decay and abandonment. Rather, since my parents last visited the hotel in the early 1990s it has been well-kept and maintained. In photographs, even beside the bright sea that spills out from the sand, the white building glistens as brightly as it always has. The land around the hotel is flat and bright. And as an aluminium sheet set through a slip roller curls, so too does that flat of desert land curve upwards from the opalescent sea to the grey ridges of the mountains around Hammamet. From a distance, the undulant crest of this slight range appears as no more than a thin swelling of darkness upwardly encroaching from some unknown face of the earth onto the wide and deboned sky, as inflamed red nodules on a pale-pink lung: aberrant and throbbing. Between the thin grey beam of mountains and the back-facing sea stand hundreds, perhaps thousands, of quadrate and domed white roofs, which from a certain height, under the bright Tunisian sun, appear like a causeway of glistening and misshapen teeth, garlanded with sun-sagged black cables and pale satellite dishes.

The hotel is housed in one such flat white building spread across two floors. The railings, doors and shutters are all painted in a Tunis blue, a bleached shade, blanched and cracked by the glaring sun and almost transparent. If you are to walk around the perimeter of the hotel, at the foot of it and scattered along the floors of the terraces, you will find flecks of light blue paint that in high winds have gently fluttered off. The rooms of the hotel face the sea, and at night residents can be seen sitting under the domed roofs that cover each terrace, quietly talking or breathing deeply in a shared silence.

On these trips, in the evenings, when the beating sun had lulled my mother to sleep, my father would spend his time at the shabby and somewhat kitsch hotel bar talking to the other guests, or out by the sea doing the same thing. There he would breathe in the saline air and pollute the desert silence with words and cigarette smoke. In 1992, my parents booked to stay a week at the Hôtel Club Riadh. By the third day, many of the guests at the hotel had left. My father would tell me in his taut and commanding voice, *There were only five guests staying: one other couple, who we thought looked Spanish and a lone, elderly Arab woman.*

My father, as he poured himself more soup from the kitchen, continued, *She wore a very long, black chador that flowed around her feet. It was quite strange and quite marvellous. The gown was frayed and torn around the hem and on one, no, two occasions, it caught beneath her sandals and she tumbled over. One time, I rushed over to help her off her knees and she didn't even look at me. But from the side I could see tears welling up in her eyes. She was frail, an old woman, and she'd drift silently through the hotel so lightly that your mother and I hardly ever heard or saw her. Sometimes, you'd catch very brief glimpses of her or see a wisp of black that you would only become aware of by the trail of fine ambergris oudh that she wore. A very fine, expensive perfume, that.*

Once my father had finished his second helping, he set his bowl to one side and lay back on his couch to go on. *One morning, your mother told me that she'd woken up in the middle of the night and had seen the old lady slowly walking back from the sea into the hotel at around midnight, maybe a little later. The two of us were stunned and curious. The next day, we decided between us to keep an eye out for her. I didn't believe your mother at first. I thought she was lying or being fantastical about it. But I was curious. The lady's presence was so spectral it could've been true. That morning, we didn't see the lady once. The room which we had assumed was hers was the only beach-front room that had its curtains tightly drawn. All the rest of the large, semi-circular windows were wide open to allow in the light and air.*

My father suddenly sat up, patted his pockets, hunted for a packet of cigarettes and finally took one, lit it then reclined back into the same sprawled position. *It was strange*, he continued. *We didn't see her around the grounds, we didn't see her in the building. I think your mother even asked the receptionist who the lady was.* My father chuckled: *She wouldn't tell us anything about that. I think that she was freaked out by us looking around and asking questions all day.*

As smoke trickled out from between my father's teeth, his hands loosely interlaced on his stomach and his cigarette growing a leaning ash, he fell into a rare moment of consideration: *I think the receptionist must've assumed something of us.*

Maybe that we posed a danger to the woman for asking her identity. I don't know. We didn't care. What was more important was that it became a part of her mystique, like she was someone who might require protection. It made her seem important to us. Your mother thought she was an old famous actress or something. Anyway. The following days passed with the mundanity holidays tend to: I would wake up late, probably hungover from the night before, and laze for hours on the balcony. Eventually, down in the food hall, I'd have the papers and take fresh fruit, yoghurt and freshly pressed carrot juice. I'm not sure when, but at some point, the hotel began to feel increasingly empty. It reminded me of being at home alone as a boy in Pakistan. I mean, we had the whole place to ourselves, he smiled, *and your mother and I relaxed, waiting for other guests to arrive but no one ever came, nor did the woman reappear. We thought she had checked out of the hotel even though her curtains were still closed.*

One night, he resumed, *I had a terrible nightmare and woke up. I dreamt that I was in my childhood home in Quetta. My bedroom there was the smallest, as it had previously been a servant's room, and in my dream I was lying there but as an adult. Downstairs, I could hear voices, lots of voices like when my parents were hosting a party or a dinner, and as I lay there unable to sleep my light mysteriously switched on. I pulled my sheet over my head, and when the voices stopped I peeked out from the covers and up above, on the ceiling, was a body dressed in all white workers' clothes hanging from the fan. I got up and ran out of the room to find my parents but the lights were all off and there was no one in the house. In fact, it was like no one had lived there for years, and along the walls, in the corners and on the furniture were cobwebs and thick layers of dust and grime. None of the lights worked and the doors outside didn't open. As I struggled to open a back door in the kitchen, I heard footsteps. I shut my eyes and waited, curled into a ball on the floor, and just as the footsteps edged right beside me I woke up in a pool of sweat beside your mother. Before I moved into that room, I was told by my older brothers, whether truthfully or teasingly, that the servant who lived there had hanged himself. For that reason, I hated sleeping in there and avoided the room during the day at all costs. At night I'd often be found outside it on the floor wrapped in a blanket or in my brother's room.*

My father paused briefly, his eyes had become pale and remote, like his boyish fear had struck him again. The dead never leave you. They remain, strangely and beautifully, sometimes horrifyingly, always surfacing, again and again above time's rising black water. It is not that you cannot escape them, it is that they never were not with you. And when you catch sight of them, even briefly, you lose sight of your present self, so through them, slowly, you join them and you dissolve with them into ranks of the past.

When I woke up, he said, present again, *I couldn't get back to sleep. I took myself out to the room's terrace with the previous day's newspaper in hand. My thinking was that sitting and reading there under the moon would help lull me back to bed. I was in a daze; half-asleep and reading about a ceasefire that had just been agreed between two warring countries. Unable to fully concentrate on the article, in the corner of my eye, at the* water's edge, I noticed a flickering light like a gas lamp. I thought I could hear talking or praying emanating from it, but I couldn't make out the words. My father's eyes suddenly enlivened: I leant forward to focus on it, this little speck of light and its sound and slowly, as my eyes adjusted to the night, I was able to make out the shape of a single body sitting by the sea. I waited on the terrace until it came closer, which it didn't for nearly two hours. I recall by that point it was close to 4 a.m. When it did at last move, it appeared to lay something down before walking back towards the hotel. The figure floated into the light with the wisps of her long black chador drifting behind her, sweeping along the ground and I realized she was carefully clutching something to her chest and holding a little tin hurricane-lantern in her hand. I stayed there for only a moment or two longer on the terrace, wondering what odd ritual I'd just witnessed.

The next morning your mother travelled to Tunis to visit Ravi, an old friend of hers who was studying nearby. She left early, long before I had woken up, and so I spent the day as I had spent the other days: by the water, in the water, in the sun, out of the sun, unwinding but really rather bored too. I walked down the beach but didn't encounter anybody, even in the midday heat. I slept a little before dinner and then sat alone at the bar watching a football match on a small television. At around 9 p.m. I decided to take dinner. The floors of the dining room were red-and-gold patterned carpet, and the tables and chairs were rimmed with scratched brass. The walls had this kind of tired, greyish tone to them which muted the room's colours. Towards the front, near the entrance, was the wood-panelled bar with entirely empty shelves, all covered in dust. The room was filled with an arboretum's worth of plants: jasmine shrubs, palms, bamboos all scattered around in chipped terracotta pots. I took a seat near the corner of the dining room facing the entrance and began to eat my dinner, a dish of houria, when the old woman entered and sat in the furthest corner, her thin body concealed by a potted fern.

She didn't have to order, he explained. Three dishes were quickly brought out without any question like it was pre-arranged. She ate with disbelief: slowly and thoughtfully and with the apprehension and awe that exists when you come from a place where people have no food at all. When she was done, she stayed to drink coffee – three cups exactly. After I finished my meal, I stood up and went over to her table. I had the newspaper under my arm, and as I approached she eyed me with a carefulness about her, a permanent suspicion. We held this moment for some seconds before she gestured for me to sit with her. As I did, she pointed at the newspaper and asked that I remove it from her sight. That was her only request, so I sat on it. She had an unforgettable face: her bones jutted out of her skin, which loosely draped off them, her large eyes were deeply set within her skull, and she had thinning but unkempt eyebrows that almost met in the middle and a thin, somewhat crooked nose. Around her eyes and across her forehead, she had crevasse-deep lines that ran through her pale brown skin like the long splits left across deserts by dead rivers and the paths of old water.

She smelt so strongly of ambergris, I thought she must've doused herself in it. Strangely, despite this, she looked dirty: her *chador was completely threadbare and torn in certain places, and her nails had collected dirt and sand beneath them. She had a total disregard for her clothing, her appearance and was someone, I felt at least, who believed that so long as she smelt acceptable then all the rest didn't matter. Being someone who dislikes silence, I spoke for probably too long. I told her about myself, your mother and our lives as she cowered in her seat, hoping to sink away from our encounter. But despite this, her eyes, soft black-grey pits, remained fixed on me like she was hanging onto each syllable with utter concentration and devotion. For what felt like hours, I rambled on and on while she sat in that corner silent and listening. And as my words began to stutter and my energy to continue talking died out, an awkward silence fell between us both, and after many minutes, under her breath, she whispered, 'I thought you were going to say something else.'*

At around midnight, my father recalled, *she rose without a word and gestured for me to follow. Out the doors of the restaurant, she drifted down to the beach, where in front of the black water and in the eye of the moon, a chair was waiting for her. Beside the chair was a lantern and a folded piece of cloth that, even in the moonlight and the lantern, wasn't at all visible under night. I helped her into the chair, and as she sat, cloaked in her thin black gown, she was absorbed into the darkness with only her yellowing teeth and the whites of her eyes reflecting the beams of the moon. We sat in silence for a moment and the old woman's eyes seemed to close. Worried she'd fall asleep, I quickly asked what brought her to this hotel, if there was a reason for her stay, if she'd ever been here before, and in that half-vanished state with her eyes firmly closed, seemingly frustrated and yet totally vulnerable, she answered in a low, hoarse Middle Eastern accent like she were intoning lines of prayer:*

I first came here, to this country, in 1904 when I was just four years old. At the time, Tunisia was what they called a French protectorate. My father was Afghani and a distant member of the ruling Barakzai family and he worked on behalf of the Afghani monarchy as an emissary to France. His wish was to establish an archaeological mission between French Tunisia and Afghanistan but due to a number of bureaucratic concerns, funding issues and logistical failures the mission wasn't established until much later, and the intervening years for my father and our family – from our first trip to the establishment of the mission – were filled with trial and strife, emptiness and anticipation.

My father began by taking my mother, my brother and I to Paris to meet with scholars and academics with his hope, and from there we'd take the train to Marseille and a boat directly to Tunis. The scholar my father worked most intimately with was a man named M. Foucher, who was particularly interested in the Krumiria region, Sousse and Nabeul, and in finding out what digs there were to be done. Following M. Foucher to Nabeul with my family was my first experience of this place.

Back then, we didn't stay at this hotel. No, this place did not exist nor did any of these places. We stayed instead at the Hôtel de France which does not exist either now. Nabeul and this country in general was so impoverished back then. The streets, of which there were few, were mostly the odd dirt path poorly separated from the other dirt paths and lined with stripped pines and high-climbing thuja. The men and women wore long-cloaked clothing and travelled by donkey. There were few cars outside of Tunis; it was mostly carts and horses. The Hôtel de France was closer to the centre of town than this hotel is and in the style of the French colonial architecture at the time. It was opulent, the only opulent building in Nabeul, and would put up passing merchants, emissaries, artists and aristocrats, all of whom arrived with the same vain and fledgling hopes of setting foot on, for them, newfound land and making something of it, imposing something into it where it was not needed, where it was not wanted, but equally where the land was too brutalized to oppose it.

During those long and hot days, where the sun slithered across the sky, my father and M. Foucher would travel to certain sites throughout the country as I, my brother Hamed and our mother all stayed at the hotel. M. Foucher believed these sites to be of importance to the study of Phoenician–Punic archaeology: tumuli, ruins of city walls, necropolis and chapels, all slowly were being whittled away by barren winds and cutting dust. M. Foucher, a meticulous and eccentric man, had extensively and thoroughly graded and listed these sites using a myriad of literary accounts, maps, obscure paintings and sketches, and his mere observation of seemingly abnormal physical indentations and protrusions in the land that, to him, were cause enough for further investigation. He would spend his evenings in the hotel working after taking dinner with our family, and upon occasion he would show Hamed and me his maps and sketches which were strewn and stacked across his desk. My brother was far more interested in the work the Frenchman was doing than I, and begin, even from a young age, to draw his own maps which were composed mostly of his childhood fantasies – ones that led to the depths of the seas, into the hearts of vast tundras and soared high above the clouds. It should be said that Hamed's cartographical passion didn't go unnoticed by M. Foucher and our father.

We would continue these same visits each year, and M. Foucher became a close companion of our family. Year after year, Nabeul, this place here, became the place we would spend our holidays. I can remember in those days, when our father was gone and our mother was lounging out of the sun, Hamed and I spent our time endlessly exploring the hotel grounds and the confines of its walls. He was curious and would make up games that would require us to search for things. There was one particular moment that no matter how hard I try, I cannot forget.

My father here explained how the elderly woman stopped: *Her lips trembled, her eyes narrowed and focused ahead on the darkness around her. She was gathering the spirit to speak or rather open a space within her to allow old spirits to speak through.*

My brother and I, she continued, *were playing a game one summer; he was chasing me through the hallways of the hotel, and as we came into the tall marble lobby I noticed a back office and ran in through it and quickly out of the workers' door into an outdoor courtyard. There were some stables, and the thick, unmoving smell of animal waste and hay hung in the air. Plugging my nose, I hid from him in an empty stable. And as Hamed crept quietly around the courtyard looking for me, a* worker and a donkey entered through the gates. Hamed stood aside. *The poor animal was panting heavily, distressed and exhausted. Its legs were shaking, it was unsteady. It had been worked through the day in the heat of the mid-summer and was dragging behind it a large cart filled with visitors' suitcases. Along the ridge of its back were deep lash marks, terrible wounds, from which a slow oozing blood matted its fur. The worker pulled at the donkey as it came closer in, and just then its knees wobbled terribly and it collapsed to the floor. The worker began to curse at it in a mixture of Arabic and French, trying to coax it up but it couldn't move.*

Soon, out rushed another worker, again attempting to pull the donkey up but it still could not move. The poor beast was so disturbed that its panting turned into what sounded like a quickened wheeze and then into an agonized wail. The two workers untied the cart from it and again together tried to lift it off the floor but in its pain it slumped onto its side. The donkey was bleeding more profusely now and made more noise. As flies buzzed around its open wounds, it kicked about on the floor, throwing up dust. The two workers together began to lash the poor thing like that would bring it to silence, but it only caused its wailing to grow louder. It writhed, attempting with whatever was left in it to move and escape the force of the blows. But it couldn't.

A Frenchman – one of the wealthy guests of the hotel – stormed out into the courtyard and reprimanded the two workers for the commotion. Upstairs, he had been holding a meeting with several Italian merchants to discuss the contracting and divvying up of certain nearby sea routes. The Frenchman re-entered the hotel again and moments later stormed back into the courtyard with a rifle, a Lebel Model 1886. He put his shiny black boot on the straining and taut animal's neck and fired a single shot squarely above its black eye.

I remember looking over to my brother who hadn't moved and was observing the scene in shock. I can still see the donkey's legs quivering as it lapsed into that last stillness. I can still see the steady stream of crimson-black pulse from the entry wound, matting the creature's fur. My brother watched it all without expression, but his eyes, wide-open and unblinking, streamed endlessly with tears. When the men left, when Hamed thought he was alone, still not knowing where I was, he threw his arms around the carcass, embracing it and shaking with grief. I would never tell him I witnessed that moment. I would instead allow him to tell me the story over and over again through the years, always emphasizing that the donkey's large glassy eye was still open and frozen forever in terror at the sight of a Frenchman with a rifle fixed on it. This moment never left my brother.

By the early 1920s, the woman went on, *my father, along with M. Foucher and the French and Afghani governments, established a delegation for archaeology in Afghanistan. From then, we saw less of M. Foucher, him being away on research trips, but my brother's interest in ancient history remained, and my father saw to it that Hamed accompanied several of his colleagues to Algeria, in particular, on digs. It was in that bruised land my brother was awakened to some fact, some fact of violence and brutality, some fact of possession and inferiority. He was an*

Afghani boy of royal descent, but to the French in Algeria he was nothing. He was little more than a pauper. An Algerian village boy. Nameless and meaningless. My brother continued his studies in History in Afghanistan and worked with the delegation my father had established. Towards the late 1930s, Hamed returned to Algeria with the threat of war casting its uncertain shadow across Europe. He would send me odd and short letters about the radio broadcasts of a ranting Austrian man that he'd listen to with the French in cafés and bars. And he'd describe the fear that was sewn into the eyes of those suited men, and also of the distant and indifferent jokes and smiles of others – remiss of a certain solemnity.

Broadcast to broadcast, the war began to flare up throughout the continent, through pointed words and failed summits. Hamed was quickly ordered back home by my mother and like a good son he obliged. When I saw him then, I could sense something within him had changed. No longer did he talk to me of formless ruins and time-covered cities, of the fine-angled shavings of Mes Aynak or the great carvings in desert walls that resembled an ancient and Eastern kind of tympanum, as he once had done. Now instead, he watched things with a cold eye and became quieter, more intense. The anonymity he felt in Algeria, the slippage of identity there allowed him to absorb their plight and had kindled an incandescent fury in him. He would tell me of the men he had seen being beaten in the street in Algiers, emaciated and helpless; of the young boys in small villages in the mountains who were sexually abused by visiting men, some notable French writers and painters of the time. He told me of the young women and girls who were subjected to rape and torture by the French authorities, and he would say this all with such unremitting and quivering rage that soon he was so entangled in his anger he'd fall short of words, resulting in an emphatic set of huffs and sighs, groans and tuts, and all throughout a silently bristling anger. Now when he argued, he spoke with a bitterness in him, sometimes even snapping at our mother and father, particularly when they applauded the French but upon other differences too, differences that would've meant little once but now seemed to place between them an ever-stretching savanna. When the war ended, without a word to any of us, Hamed slinked back off to Algeria.

We wouldn't hear from him for many months. Sometimes the occasional letter or telegram would arrive, sometimes a call. But no matter what, our infrequent communication became inevitably brief. He remained in Algeria for years, and by 1946 we lost contact with him entirely. The last letter he sent simply read: 'All's well. Will be quiet for a bit. Thinking of you all, of course. H.' By then, our father and mother were coming close to death and both were sick with worry. My father ordered people, his trusted Frenchmen he knew in Algeria who worked for the government and authorities, to seek Hamed out but not one search resulted in any lead. He asked locals he knew there to look and heard nothing other than whispers and quiet intonations of the vaguest of possibilities. In 1949, both my parents passed within six months of each other, and even then Hamed didn't rear his head, nor did they pass into the next life knowing what had happened to their son. His quietness remained for many years and an unanswered quietness is often loudest within yourself. I couldn't escape its noise and looked for him endlessly following our parents' death. He was the last remaining member of my family. I spent months travelling through Algeria, Maroc and Tunisia looking for him and never came close to learning anything. I notified the Algerian authorities and they too, in the midst of great upheaval, came up short. There was nothing. It was as though Hamed had vanished entirely without leaving so much as a shadow behind him. It seemed he lived without connections, without relation-ships, without any work and without so much as a foot upon a paver. I didn't believe it and stupidly, naively, held on to the loose possibility that one day he might reappear. But after so long hoping, after almost two decades, when the possibility had all but vanished and Hamed only presented himself to me in dreams and in nightmares, in odd occurrences on the street when I saw someone I thought might be him, or when I mistook a stranger's voice for his; when memories of him arose in my mind from the sight of a picture of him – Hamed had become all but hidden in me, a fiction in my mind, nothing more than a buried figure of the past I had forgotten the face of.

In the early 1960s, I was living in London and conducting research at the British Museum on behalf of my father's organ-ization. One night, there was a knock at my door. It was snowing outside and my apartment on Philbeach Gardens was without much heating. I had been listening to the news beside one of those old electric heaters with a blanket pulled over my knees. I reluctantly answered, and at my door arrived a shivering young woman. She had a brown paper parcel held tightly to her chest and her left hand was missing its ring finger. Her teeth chattered madly. She only spoke my name and then asked, 'It's you, yes?' I invited her in and made tea. I can still see the woman's eyes, still picture them burning green, tender yet feral. She had a complexion not so unlike our own, lighter perhaps but a beautiful tone that was reddened from the cold weather. Her hair was black and cropped. She had an air of unease about her. As she warmed, she spoke with an Algerian accent muddied with French and eventually explained her story to me:

'In my home in Algeria, I fought on the side of the resistance. First with the CRUA and later with the FLN. I ran communications between different operations in the Aurès region and Kabylia. And in Béjaïa, in the late 1940s I met your brother, Hamed. For so long there were rumblings in the way of independence and resistance, and I sought out your brother having been told that he was an important voice in support of the struggle of my people. Through those few years, your brother and I worked closely on a number of demonstrations, insurgency campaigns and assassinations. These were acts that even now alone with you in London, I fear to detail aloud.'

The shivering woman, the old woman explained, *then told me that in 1958 she and Hamed were captured and taken prisoner by the French. She was only released after being subjected to a prolonged period of torture by them, including the severing of her finger, electrocution, sexual abuse and sleep deprivation. Soon after, she fled for Tangier and eventually landed in Spain, fearing for her safety and to recover from her injuries. The young woman explained that the French believed she and Hamed were lovers, and to prevent him from ever marrying her they cut off her ring finger. The young woman never knew for certain what end Hamed met but on a boat out of Oran one night she was told by someone who claimed to have known Hamed that he, along with twenty or thirty others, with their heads covered and their feet cast in concrete, were dropped from a plane into the sea near the Algerian–Tunisian border by the French military.*

As the young woman explained this all to Hamed's sister, things slowly erased in her: grievances, hatred for her brother's silence, her pain and disorder. With the stranger's words, things loosened in her, and in their place was left blankness, emptiness, a deep chasm of emotion that instead of being filled was erased, leaving in her a vacuum that eviscerated any entering thought or memory.

The young woman then handed her the parcel and explained it was a *ghlila djabadouli*, a traditional Algerian jacket that Hamed had owned. Hamed's sister received the jacket, shaking, and slowly unwrapped it. *The old woman recalled,* my father said, *that when she first saw it, she was shocked by how austere it was for a traditionally ornate jacket, and then was jarred, so disturbed by it that she dropped it to the floor like she had felt something brush past her. She left it on the floor for some time, refusing to pick it up.*

The young woman, the stranger, told Hamed's sister that when she was released by the French, she went to find Hamed at his residence and only found the jacket which had been left at the back of his wardrobe. The rest of his belongings had been seized or destroyed. Afterwards, the two women were both at a loss and consumed by knotted thoughts, basic and complex questions that words could never ease and, above all else, ceaseless visions of Hamed and those other prisoners falling through the night to their deaths. Despite offers by Hamed's sister, the young woman left before washing, eating or sleeping, and not long after she had departed and the last of the snowy air in the apartment warmed, Hamed's sister gently dozed off beside the electric heater with her late brother's *ghlila* draped over her shoulders. As she slipped into dreams, her head lolling off into sleep, in that slender moment, images and memories of her brother slowly flooded her mind, and as sleep finally consumed her tired head she saw him once more from the empty stable – a young boy, expressionless and utterly still, weeping between the dense shadows of powerlessness and fury.

She didn't become upset, my father recalled, *when explaining any of this to me. By then, she had found a comfort in knowing of her brother's death and more so of his life. That night by the sea in Nabeul, she showed me the cloth that she always held with her, and doubtless, it was Hamed's* ghlila. *However, unlike how she had first explained seeing it – austere and navy – it was woven with various intricate patterned patches and vivid colours. The patches made up the shell of the jacket and it was transformed into a kaleidoscope of contrasting colour and design. Some of the patches were shoddily sewn in and others were unsewn with exposed threading loose and hanging off the coat. It was an ever-evolving work – a ceaseless canvas.*

Each year, my father continued, *she would come to Nabeul and stay at the Hôtel Club Riadh. And on each night of her stay, she would sit by the water and proceed to unstitch all the patches from the previous year to restitch a set of new colours and patterns into her brother's old jacket. She would spend part of the year before sourcing new materials, attempting to create an entirely new piece of clothing each year. The only constant colour was that derived from the dye of the damask rose, a dye native to Nabeul. This process, continuous and shifting, she believed kept her in close conversation with Hamed. It was a ritual I struggled to understand but what I did realize is that it was her way of keeping the past near her.*

After she finished her story, the elderly woman sternly asked my father to leave her alone by the water, as by night, while she stitched, in not more than a whisper she would talk to Hamed in the dim gleam of her lamp's light as the black waves folded, the moon bulged and crumbled into day and her questions were met with the same silence that had always greeted them.

I recall after my father stopped his story, he sat wordless, thoughtless, seemingly trying to recapture his mind from where his words had taken him. Outside his apartment, tucked safely down Bramley Road, through his windows, shadows of figures flashed onto his walls, cars picked up drizzle from the tarmac, and passing voices seeped into the space before vanishing once more down the road's distance. As night drew out along the world and his apartment darkened, I watched my father – slight and gaunt, nestled between two sofa cushions – dim into nothing more than a half-shadow which cigarette smoke trickled from the mouth of. I don't know how long we stayed there in each other's company nor what my father's expression was, nor even what he said to me before I left that night.

After these long moments of recollection in my studio, the contour of my father's shadow would remain scarred on the inside of my eyelids. Each time I looked around I would see him sat there with me. Each time I blinked, I was with him again until the scarring healed and the image of him faded and there was nothing, only darkness. Once my mind fell to rest, slowly in that dark studio, in that strange town, miles from all I knew, the rush of the waves and the soughing reeds on the water's edge would gradually sound again; the dry smell of salty air and bitter spume would slowly enter my nostrils and the sound of boats on the pier would fill the studio, and steadily from the ends of my memory I would reappear. Present again, there in that space as all those thoughts: the images of my father so many years prior, the bleached and ravaged land of Tunisia and the thought of Hamed's jacket, stitched and restitched, re-patterned and reformed, all receded into the depths of my mind and upwards from beneath time's black water, through the unending greyness, from over the whitish and shorn hills and through the mist of spring rains, I appeared but only for a short period of time before I vanished again beneath the distant and echoing words of another elsewhere.

In this pendulous movement, from the daintiest of threads,

between absence and presence, between voice and erasure, I am reminded of people and spaces, names and dates, all as words to which I listened. And now, like those distant and ancient spirits from the East who once moved above gardens as ghostly stewards of the birds and the trees, I am free to float back through them. Floating so silently, without ever having to utter a word. Only to inspect, once more, those who lingered on the sharp edge of a shattering scream and a heavy silence before being erased forever by the dark clouds of oblivion, by the swirling hurricanes of time, by the deluge of ashen rain, by the gentle and continual stilling of motion. But as always, before this process commences, like passing ships in the night, a glint of their light can be caught in the distance, can be fixed upon for only a moment, before again they fall to the bottom of time's black water where they're drowned and the surface of the water becomes still again, still as though they were never there to begin with.

Last autumn, when I was renting a cabin in Northfield, a small town on the border of Massachusetts and Vermont, as I do each year, I received a call from an old friend named Daphne who told me that her father, a longtime friend of my mother, as well as our family doctor in Oxford, had suffered a brain haemorrhage on a beach in Cyprus and passed away. All that she said to me was, *It was sudden . . . In the middle of the day . . . Reading on Cessac Beach . . . No, he was alone.*

Following his retirement, Dr Otto Canning persisted, as he had when he was working, in spending part of autumn in the same small village of Ormideia in the north-east of Cyprus, whereas in the summer months, he'd remain in his tall and narrow terraced home at the bottom of Walton Well Road in the Oxford suburb of Jericho. As consistent as he was in his appearance – stiff and balding; his hair cropped to the exact same centimetre and wearing the same wire-framed black glasses, which he pushed up to rest in the exact same position on his angular prow of a nose every few minutes – he was in his choosing of the month of his holiday. Each year, he was always, and somewhat mysteriously, away for the entire month of October, and across those same years, this specific and recurring choice of both time and obscure destination became something to speculate over for us.

When eventually Dr Canning would return from his holiday, it was never with stories or pictures, reasons or answers, but instead – after handing back to my mother the book she had given him to read while away, or sometimes forgetting to – he'd arrive back with only taciturn responses to her probing: *Good, Enjoyable, Relaxing*, along with a telling half-grin and a deep-set tan, so uniform and unbroken in tone, it was similar to that of a labourer, or a farmer.

After first having returned from Boston, before my mother's illness became so severe she was unable to even so much as leave the house, as it had been when I bumped into Mr Rothlan, I would often accompany her to the limestone terraced house where Dr Canning kept his surgery. Although she knew each year in October, Dr Canning, along with his wife, Claire – before her death – would be away in that small fishing village in Cyprus, whenever the two of us arrived at his practice and were greeted by a different doctor because, *D. Canning is on holiday*, she would turn to me and ask, with a choked kind of a smile, *Why does he always go to that strange little village?*

It was that same autumn when Daphne first told me the story, two decades ago now, at the point in the season in which summer and the warmth of its breeze – although still close enough to be sensible – has entirely taken leave, and there emerged the hoarfrost needles of an impending winter-frost chiming ever so quietly in the air. We were sat in the stone courtyard of a low-beamed pub in the centre of the city, down a dimly lit street call Hollymead. The pub was busy, and the ancient-seeming, slanted walls that surrounded it caused the noise of other punters to pool around us. We had both ended up back in Oxford, as young adults so often return home soon after briefly venturing out into the world; I, having returned from Boston, felt as equally lost as Daphne, a talented cellist who in the months prior to our meeting had been auditioning – unsuccessfully – for conservatoires in London and Scotland, and after trying and failing, ended up returning home. Later, she went on to play with the Munich Philharmonic and later the Freiburg.

Our meeting in the pub had come after one of those mornings where my mother looked at me in the waiting room of her doctor's office with a hidden smile and asked that same question about that same odd village; a question which, at the point of her asking, I truly didn't know the answer to.

If you are to look at a map, you can see that the village of Ormideia sits within and on a number of borders. It is an exclave of Akrotiri and Dhekelia – a British Overseas Territory made up of military bases, which itself borders the demilitarized buffer zone – or the Green Line, as it is colloquially known, as well as Northern Cyprus. While I myself never visited Ormideia, and Cyprus only once, I have seen pictures of the flat and rocky coast there, as well as the scantly dotted flat-roofed white houses, quadrate and with open windows showing into darkened rooms. I have seen the short stone piers, surrounded by gnarls of rough shrubbery, with blanched blue boats tethered to stone posts, and I have often tried to envisage what it was that that genial and reticent man found in that village so far from the usual sights of Cyprus, and pressed between buffer zones and military installations, between regions recognized and regions unrecognized, and all the while vacating itself of all those words and in fact pertaining to none of it at all.

Daphne told me how her father persisted in visiting this same small village in the coastal north of the Larnaca district, as it was where he and Claire – when young – had once got stuck after attempting to drive from the south-western city of Paphos up to Famagusta in the north in a faulty white rental that broke down just outside of that very village. They were forced to stay there overnight, as due to the remoteness of Ormideia there wouldn't be anyone to help repair their car, or even to give them a lift back to Paphos until the next morning.

The young couple had found their white rental sputtering to a halt on a straight of pot-holed road with a tall pine tree on either side: one that was dead, its bark pale and ashy; the other, verdant with a darker bark and lighter brown patches of tree revealed beneath. It was a two-lane road; the white of its dividing line cracked, with flat and rocky land flaring out on both sides. Slightly ahead of them, in the near distance, behind a rail of shrubs, the walls and roofs of houses, was the sea.

There was the smell, as Dr Canning would recall later to Daphne, who in the garden of the pub recounted to me as being *A bitter mixture of the sea and the plants*; the weighty scent of the salt-stung air and sun-baked flora, from which effused the raw pheromones of the thick and sagging leaves of wild olive trees and fumana; there was also the heat, which by that point in the afternoon had reached a withering level, prompting them to make for the village.

The young couple removed their bikes and belongings from the car, locked it, and cycled on together. As they drifted past the white houses, they looked through the windows, whose slatted shutters were swung open against the exterior walls, lain flat like sleeping dogs in thick beams of sunlight, and all the houses were apparently empty; they saw nothing but vacant kitchens or silent living rooms, a seemingly uninhabited village. They cycled on further down a narrow lane, passing unoccupied stoops outside front doors, that they would later learn was where, in the mornings, the villagers would sit, smoke cigarettes, drink from handleless, pale-yellow coffee mugs and converse loudly with each other.

Eventually, the pair passed into the village square, at the centre of which stood a large fountain surrounded by dozens of occupied benches and where, suddenly, all the villagers appeared like apparitions, talking and laughing with one another above the gentle babble of the fountain into its leaf-filled pool.

After explaining their situation to a group of three locals – two women and a man – who were sat closest to where they entered, the man, who introduced himself as Nico, and had a lazy left eye, called over to his friends – two darker-skinned men – who were crookedly stooped on an opposite bench smoking and talking in solemn and agreeable-sounding tones, and relayed their situation. Together with Dr Canning and Claire, a group of three old Cypriot men, dressed in short-sleeved cotton shirts, and workman shorts, went off and inspected the car, which consisted largely of the old men, bending over like three birds pecking at grains, wandering around the outside, trying to peer beneath the chassis – together, they explained it couldn't be fixed until the next morning, seeing as the mechanic was in another town visiting his mother, but would likely return early the next day. Duly, Nico led them back to the square, wherefrom the pair met again with the two women, one of whom, after Nico explained their situation, invited the young doctor and his wife to stay in her home for the night.

As Dr Canning would recall to Daphne, the couple agreed. The woman, who introduced herself as Elif, explained that Nico was a Greek-Cypriot and the two other men were Turkish-Cypriot, like her. Dr Canning and Claire dropped their things in a spare room before, at last, setting off on their bikes down the route along the coast they had initially intended to cycle.

Once they had passed a thin line of pine trees, they reached a low scrubland, a phrygana of sorts, at the end of which the opal ocean appeared. Upon reaching the shore, they banked north and cycled on past the stone pier, which at that time was empty of both boats and people. From along the seawall, they spotted the profile of a dozen or so boats only a few hundred metres out at sea, with the silhouettes of narrow and angular figures casting nets into the water and dragging them in again rather quickly. They continued on the path of the seawall for an hour, perhaps two, cycling further away from the village of Ormideia and into that rugged and harsh land, one whose topology was assuaged by the milky wind billowing against their clothes and the hollow frames of the bicycles, and the view of the sea which darkened and lightened under the fast passing of clouds sailing inland. It didn't seem long before this spell was broken and they found themselves at the end of the path facing a tall chain-link fence with a sign which read:

BUFFER ZONE

NO PHOTOS

Through the fence they could see what appeared as the same plain of land that was behind them, it was almost directly replicative of the journey they'd already taken, only severed by the steely interlocking metal into individual elements, of the same alien-seeming sights that for the past two hours had stunned them into a joint and mystified silence. At the fence, the side of captivity and the side of freedom, which portion of land was being kept from the other was not clear to them, nor truly the reasons why.

After reaching that point of their journey, with the sun beginning its slow descent in the sky, like it were the rock in a sling being dragged down by a child's hand, they turned around and began to cycle back towards the village. When eventually they reached the stone pier again, they saw that the boats were coming in. Some were already tied to the stone posts and hauling their catch into large crates. A dense cloud lumbered across the sky, casting the landscape into a shimmering and forbidding shadow.

It was here in the story of her parents that Daphne told me how in July 1958 a Greek-Cypriot woman named Calliope, pregnant with a girl, hoping to escape the ethnic violence, abandoned the island of Cyprus without the father of her child. *A dirty dog*, as she'd call him, or rather, a Turkish man named Mehmet. Somewhat bewildered and completely spent after those long hours waiting in the terminal of Nicosia Airport, she arrived at London Heathrow, which she did with no more than a single large suitcase. She was helped through to a taxi outside by a young attendant, no older than nineteen, with long brown hair, dark eyes and who, once outside the terminal, Calliope stood and sobbed into the shoulder of. When she asked the attendant's name, it was the same that she'd later give to her daughter.

A month after Calliope had arrived in London she gave birth. And the little girl, despite her pale-white English namesake, was born with dark and curly hair, and a deep-beige complexion like she had emerged from the womb of the sun. She and her mother spent the first ten months of their existence in West London in a small room in Calliope's brother's apartment in Hanwell. Calliope found work as a hairdresser in Acton, and the baby, Claire, was raised in the care of her aunt in the day and her mother at night. Once Calliope had saved enough money for their own place, mother and daughter moved just down the road to Ealing where Claire began school.

Claire never entirely resolved her father's identity from her mother. She recounted later, to her own daughter, Daphne, the unease she felt at even so much as the thought of mentioning him in front of Calliope. *Every time she brought him up*, as Daphne told me, *my nana flew into a rage, or instead, she'd leave the room.* The young Claire would console her mother then, as she called him, *A dog*, or when she was particularly incensed by some hidden and insuperable thought of him, *A dirty rotten pig.* Claire having never known her father, grew up without a thought of him beyond him being a dog, and sometimes a pig, which naturally caused in her, according to Daphne, *An urge to betray her mother. Whatever she didn't know about him, she made up, and what she made up was the opposite of whatever my nana hinted about him.*

Daphne told me how when Claire was a girl she had one notebook in which she wrote out letters from her father to her; letters where he would detail where he was, when he'd be back and talk about his own childhood. While I never was able to read the letters, nor heard in much detail of their contents, the image of the young Claire, hiding away in the bedroom in the basement apartment in Ealing, stashing away from her mother those fictitious letters, always coloured my idea of her.

I was too young to remember how I perceived Claire, having only met her when I was a child. Though I do remember one night, when I was somewhat older, not long before Claire passed, being sat downstairs in the kitchen when my mother came home from dinner, having been dropped off by Claire. She had arrived earlier than I thought she might, and as I saw the headlights of the car flash through the blinds of the kitchen window, I looked up, taken aback. Through the window, rather vaguely too, I saw my mother and Claire sat in the crude glow of the car's overhead light, seemingly both in silence. My mother was turned away, and yet I could tell that she was listening; while Claire, whose face appeared so removed and lifeless beneath that nauseating light, which to me had the ability to reveal all the marks of time, was speaking. Her mouth moved very slightly, as though she was whispering, and in a manner that was so delicate, I couldn't tell if it was, in fact, a trick of the mind. Only when I saw my mother nod did I realize she must be talking.

My mother entered the house with her head bowed and a look of abstraction drawn across her face. Her eyes were narrowed but blank. It was not distance I noticed her absent-mindedly enter with, but rather an interior kind of close attention. When, eventually, she noticed me sat there looking at her, she paused for a few seconds then slowly said: *Poor Claire*, elongating each syllable, as though tipsily stumbling from her thoughts, with half an eye still on them. Although I never asked my mother what it was that she meant, I saw within her the inflamed wound of another having been drawn across her eyes, which seemed to dim with each further step into her home. That night, my mother shut herself away in her room, and I sat beneath, listening for her footsteps, of which I heard not one.

It was at Bristol University they met, Daphne told me in answer to a question of mine. *She was eighteen, studying law and Dad was a year older, studying medicine. When Dad was twenty-six and Mum was twenty-five they married. They lived in Clifton at first, in the attic of a man named Mr Hammel.* I knew through my mother that, by then, Claire had begun work as a clerk at an old London firm called Nagle & Thompson based in Bloomsbury that specialized in human rights law. Each morning, she would take the train from Platform 5 in Temple Meads to Paddington.

She would always tell me, Daphne said, *whenever she was walking along the platform, beneath the arching train-shed roof, how she was haunted by an old local legend that had been recounted by Mr Hammel upon first hearing her name.*

In late 1917, when boarding a train to return to the trenches in France, Private Douglas Selby was told by his wife, Claire, that she was pregnant by another man. Selby, upon hearing this, unslung his rifle from his shoulder and shot her dead there on the platform. Private Selby, without any kind of resistance, then handed himself over and was quickly tried and executed for the murder. This story had remained with Claire, according to Daphne, and simply so for the image that was conjured of Selby, rather coldly, without any presence of emotion, killing the woman he loved before then submitting himself to the same inescapable fate.

Even now, as I could during the night in the pub with Daphne, so long ago now, I can imagine Claire stood among a gallery of similarly tired and bedraggled commuter faces, as a winter wind blew in heaves down the platform, and how she might too have thought, just as I have, that what Selby did was not some freak aberration, but perhaps, in a sense, what commonly happens, not as violently and as publicly, but instead quietly and gradually, across the long span of years and decades.

According to Daphne, whenever they returned to Bristol as a family, often by train, Claire would point out the platform and repeat this tale to her: *She never said it in a jovial manner. She always seemed disturbed by it. And she would tell it again and again, even when I would say to her, 'You've already told me this story.'*

After two years of sedulous work at Nagle & Thompson, across a number of cases, which spanned the continent of Africa, Bangladesh, Northern Ireland and Palestine, and taking time in between to visit her mother in Ealing on the weekends, sometimes staying in her childhood bedroom if her work ran on too late, one morning at work she found herself confronted by something that had, until that point at least, been neatly crimped away in her.

When she reached this point of her mother's story, Daphne leaned backward in her chair and took a deep sip of her drink. I remember the voices around us in the pub that night seemed to louden and drown out Daphne's voice, and it took me several seconds, perhaps more, to realize that Daphne had, in fact, stopped talking altogether. She looked at me intensely with short, pinhole eyes. Her silence dragged on until I eventually summoned the courage to prompt her into continuing; she then recounted to me what her mother had told her countless times, years before: *My mother was handed a file on the case of an old Cypriot man, a former schoolteacher who for many years had been hoping to sue the Turkish government. This was because early one morning – more than two decades before – the man had been disturbed by the sounds of shouting outside his home in central Cyprus. He looked through his window and saw a dozen or so soldiers banging on the doors. And almost as soon as he looked through the window, the man heard banging on his own door and shouting in a language he recognized as Turkish from broadcasts of Ecevit and Erbakan on the news and the radio.*

Daphne, whose eyes brightened with each further fall into her memory of it, told of how in the time between the man looking out of his window and seeing the band of Turkish soldiers in dark green fatigues and him treading carefully through his bedroom, past his upright wife, who looked at him with dark and startled eyes, and reaching his front door, most of their neighbours had also opened their doors, some without shirts, all still wiping away the sleep from their eyes, and were looking at the soldiers, who had continued on down the narrow lane of houses.

Daphne shook her head, in the way that she did when she was trying to expel some other train of thought from upending her current one. There had always been something rhythmic about the way Daphne talked, something both authoritative, solemn and still, as if she were distracted, like despite her speaking, there was something else she was listening to. We often joked about it when we were children. There was seemingly some other sound that was more important than her own voice, unheard to the rest of us and apparently playing perpetually. Speaking then, for her, was a constant battle with the sound of her own interior self. She one day told me that she struggled to be in crowded spaces for the sensitivity of her ears, which seemed – no matter how she tried to resist it – to take in each and every other sound that played around her. I have heard of this since in other musicians, and as well, in a gardener I once knew. To my shame, it has taken me all this time to see it was not her own inner self she was trying not to hear, but the world around her.

Despite this, sometimes, she succeeded in doing so and was able to continue with what her thoughts were: *The Cypriot man, who was stood in his door frame, shouted across to his neighbour, a friend of his, asking what was happening. But at that moment, one of the soldiers, a young man, no older than seventeen years probably, turned around and began yelling at them again. But this time, the young man who was 'no more than a boy'* [as was written in the old schoolteacher's testimony] *seethed. Angrily, he approached them then pointed his rifle at them. All the men stuck their hands in their hair and stepped out from their houses and walked ahead of the boy.*

Beyond the details of the story which Daphne described to me, I sensed the years and years of her mother telling and re-telling the story to her daughter, or to audiences around their kitchen table, until eventually the story no longer became a trifle that Daphne, as a young girl, would listen to with her head sleepily resting on her father's hand, which beneath her warm cheek rested on the wooden table, concealing a small pile of crumbs he'd gathered; rather, it was a story as stiff and as straight as his posture was in those moments, as scarlet as his pursed lips, and as still as his eyes upon his wife, despite him having heard the story dozens, if not hundreds of times, before; it was a story that became a way for her to obliquely trace, as a blind man would with a trembling finger, the contours of the vague and ambiguous parts she sensed within herself, and her recital of the story rendered those same hollows unmistakably yet oddly clear to her. As with photographic light-leaks, the image is not destroyed but instead remade into an image where distortion not precision matters, where the mist cleanses. As I recall reading somewhere in an old book of poetry, *The lights would not be visible if they did not have the fog to break through.*

The men, as Daphne told me, *were led north out of the village.* The soldiers had surrounded them, and the menacing boy with black and empty eyes stood alone behind them, prodding them onward into the wilderness. Halfway up a craggy incline they eventually reached a shepherd's hut that all the men knew well, for it having been owned and inhabited by one of the Turkish-Cypriot farmers named Yusuf, who had leased it from a Greek landowner.

As they were led up the incline, whenever one of the men turned around to look back onto the village they had just been forced from, the boy, who was stood stoutly behind them, shouted insensible words at them, words that by virtue of the vehemence with which they were spat, pronounced themselves as slurs, or threats, despite the men not knowing as much. When one of the other soldiers at the back hushed the boy, the only one who had his gun raised, the boy began crying, *Mustafa. Mathiatis. Mustafa! Mathiatis!* It was then that the old schoolteacher knew what it was that caused the graveness and irascibility in the boy's encumbered eyes, or at least provided him with the crucial word to see the wellspring of the boy's fury.

Mathiatis had been a small farming village of a few hundred people, just twenty miles south of Cyprus's severed capital city, Nicosia, and it was comprised of a near-equal split of Turkish- and Greek-Cypriots. In the spring and summer, Greek landowners leased the surrounding hills and pasture to Turkish shepherds; in the village market, fruits and vegetables harvested, or imported, were sold in the square. In 1963, near to Christmas by only a matter of days, hundreds of militant Greek youths, all armed, with a squadron of policemen in tow, descended upon the Turkish quarter of the village. They began indiscriminately firing rifles into the houses as the Turkish residents fled and used torches to burn down the wood-beamed white houses.

As Claire had read in the testimony, upon hearing the name of the village, the old schoolteacher assumed then that the boy-solider was referring to the massacre there and thought that the name Mustafa must've been that of a relative, perhaps a brother, or a father.

Upon reaching the doors of the shepherd's hut, the men – no more than twelve in number – were packed in. Though the hut had been cleared of any animals, still in the cool clay corners were collected small piles of yellowing and grass-tangled fur, some matted tufts that had, some time before, been sheared off. The uneven floor bore traces of smeared blood, and the schoolteacher wondered, momentarily, if it was the blood of Yusuf, who he hadn't seen in some days. In his testimony, the schoolteacher wasn't able to give an exact time as to when he was woken by the soldiers, nor was he able to recall how long exactly it was that they were all kept huddled in that hut. With the door closed behind them, only so much as a fleck of light was visible, which came through a crack, not more than a centimetre wide, in the clay wall beside where the old schoolteacher stood. Through it, he was only able to make out the arid turf outside.

At first the men stood in silence, having been shushed. Some closed their eyes, craned their necks forward and whispered prayers, *All-merciful . . . Become flesh to save all.* Outside the hut, the sound of voices, no more than mutterings, lasted for a while then a few dozen boots crunching against the dirt drifted off somewhere into the distance. The schoolteacher, through the narrow aperture, was able to make out that one, perhaps two of the soldiers had remained outside. He imagined it was the young boy, although he couldn't say for certain. After several hours, some of the captives slid down the walls and fell into hunched positions on the damp floor. Despite the coolness of the small hut when they had first entered, the heat outside, along with the heat of the men's bodies, had caused the cramped space to become unbearable. One of the men began to hyperventilate, while another banged against the door, trying to force it open; all the while, the schoolteacher remained standing, looking through the aperture, and seeing that the day had grown into afternoon, and by all appearances, the one, perhaps two soldiers were no longer outside the walls of the hut. He dared not mention it, purely out of fear that he might provoke one of the other men to try and break free from the enclosure and cause a sleeping guard, perhaps the boy-soldier, to punish them all duly for the violation.

After many hours, when the crack in the aperture filled not with light but an indigo shade, and the earth outside of the hut became no more perceptible than the wandering half-shadows of the phantasmic possibility of soldiers, one of the men, from out of the shared agonized silence, began at random to tell the stories of his grandfather, Christos, who had once travelled to London to visit his cousin, and spent the rest of his years talking about his time there, about his fantastical idea of the place that was seared so deeply in his mind. Claire read in the old Greek man's testimony about how the captive few, with rapt attention – although exhausted, famished and sweltering – listened to the tales of the man's grandfather, who had stayed at the Marion Lodge in Haringey under the care of a Ms Manning – an Irish exile – and at night he walked the streets of Piccadilly and Bloomsbury, St James and down to Albert Bridge, which he wandered towards in a trance, taken by the reflection of its glittering lights on the black water, before returning to a cup of tea and a slice of ginger cake prepared and left by Ms Manning on the downstairs table, on a plate, covered by a bowl.

As Daphne told me, the man's talking provoked a soldier to swing open the door. Despite not being able to entirely make out the face of the soldier, the men knew by the sound of his voice that it was, naturally, the boy who had driven them on. Again, he hushed them bitterly and locked the door. The schoolteacher, once more, peered through the crack in the wall into the purplish night. There he saw a gentle flickering outside, as though the embers of dozens of cigarettes were being pulled upon at once, which – as he described in his testimony – took him several minutes to realize was not an illusion brought on by his delirious exhaustion, but rather the sudden appearance of hundreds of fireflies. His acknowledgement of them came with their steady proliferation, and like the stars slowly coming into view studding a clear night-sky, they dramatically glittered against the shaded land.

The old schoolteacher remained upright against the wall looking through the aperture, watching the dancing of the fireflies, until the sound of a dozen or so boots approaching on the dry earth came to his ears, and the door was swung open. The men were led out at the orders of an older soldier and marched over the craggy incline. Many stumbled upon each other, as they were forced to march in close single file. Once they reached the other side of the incline, they were pushed onto their knees. Ahead of them, down below, were twelve villages and settlements, lit up and speckled against the dark floor of the island, scintillant, seemingly vibrating.

After Claire read through the testimony in the file, she asked to meet the old Cypriot. The following week he came into the offices of Nagle & Thompson, where after some time talking, he showed her the scars along his back and across his arms. He talked of how he wanted to sue the Turkish government for damages, and that he could no longer stand even being near Turkish people, for they were a bunch of *Damn dirty dogs!* Words that caused something of a paralysis in Claire, who so desperately wanted to respond, even as much as to reveal her own heritage, however severed and incomplete it felt in her, and yet, she found herself unable and simply nodded at him.

It was something she was always ashamed of, as Daphne told me, *that she couldn't say anything to defend herself. It felt dishonest. But the guilt afterwards was too much for her to bear. And so, she passed on the man's case to somebody else. Citing a conflict of interest.* The following year, Dr Canning found work in

Oxford, and so the couple moved from Mr Hammel's attic flat to their home in Oxford. This, in turn, brought Claire closer to London, her work and to Calliope.

When I was younger, in a bid to allay my frenzied energy, my mother would often walk me through the parks and meadows of the city. She would lead me down the footpath alongside the river, over Folly Bridge, down the meadow walk, over into the orchard or Aston's Eyot. Along this same route, we would frequently see Dr Canning, either alongside Claire or alone. As I remember it, they were often on their bicycles. And it became something of a joke to Daphne about how her father and mother enjoyed to cycle, *More than they enjoyed spending time with me!* She told me of how her grandmother, Dr Canning's mother, would tell of the young and shy Otto, who would cycle endlessly around Stowmarket where he had grown up. It was a passion of his he took into his schooldays, later his university, which is where one summer he and two friends cycled from Calais to Monaco – something that Daphne explained the doctor, who rarely spoke at length, ceaselessly talked about to her.

Many times had I heard the story of how when he first met Claire at Bristol she hadn't learnt to ride a bike, nor even so much as sat on one. During their university days, the two of them would sneak off to St George Park and he would teach her. And quietly, that first summer break, she borrowed her cousin's bike and continued to practise riding near her mother's home in Ealing. Then the two of them would spend weekends away cycling through the country, along the coast, in both Pembrokeshire and Exmoor. Once they moved to Oxford, and in a time when she took leave from work, Claire would only ever be spotted on her bike, and later, with Daphne strapped to a plastic chair above her back tire.

Two years before having Daphne, just weeks after meeting the old Cypriot man, who had shown Claire the deep welts across his arms and scarring across his shoulders, she asked her husband if together they could visit Cyprus, a place she had never so much as found it in her to consider travelling to, but driven by the words of an incensed man, which only echoed her mother's, she felt suddenly impelled to see and breathe the country for herself.

It had been Dr Canning who mapped a number of cycling routes out, many of which hugged the coast, and so it was the result, in Daphne's words, of *his overambition*, that had led to the two of them, one night, sharing a single bed in the house of a tall and tanned woman named Elif.

In the days prior to their arriving fortuitously in Ormideia, they had been staying at a lodge in Paphos; something that, Daphne recalled, *My mother didn't enjoy*, as just two days before they had arrived, they heard a story about a young Lebanese boy, only several streets down from where they were staying, being chased from his work and beaten senseless by a group of men who, it was reported, yelled *Pig* at him, having mistaken him to be Turkish.

My mother felt because of her darker skin and her thick curly hair she was being looked at scornfully. She felt uncomfortable in certain bars and restaurants, and repeatedly explained to my dad how she would like to spend more time in the north. That was one of the reasons that the two of them ended up driving so far to cycle.

The next morning, after waking up and being given breakfast and coffee, Dr Canning and Claire again cycled the same route they had the afternoon before: down to the sea, left past the stone pier, along the coast and unmarked barren paths, up to the fence of the Green Line that divided the north and the south of the island. I imagine, as Dr Canning looked all around, Claire remained peering through the fence onto the other portion of land, and thought there of her father, whose name she never resolved, nor who she discovered anything about. She only ever heard him referred to as *a dog*, or *a pig*, nothing more or less. I like to imagine at the fence, for some reason, she was able to reflect upon those slurs, and imagined where it was in herself, or rather which part of herself – beyond the darker shade of beige, or the added thickness and kink in her hair – existed on the other side; rather, which part of the rocky and prohibited landscape existed in her; if it was as simple as that; if her own notion of herself could adequately exist without a complete knowledge of it, or if, in fact, it didn't matter to know more, nor did it matter to acquire a record of her hidden half. She feared that her dis-coveries – if she were ever to make them – beyond being mere fantasies, might fail to affect the sum of herself, as what it was she had hoped to discover was submerged, suppressed and forgotten, and despite her sense that, perhaps, on the other side of the chain-link fence she stared through, there was some answer, she also was aware of the fact that she could – if she so wanted – cross that line and go in search of it; and yet, throughout the remainder of her life, she never did.

Instead, each year, she asked her husband that they return to the exclave, the fishing village they had fortuitously fallen upon, which was within partitioned land, not far from the border. Two years later, they brought their newborn daughter named Daphne with them, whose middle name is Elif, after the woman who insisted that every time they visited they came for dinner at her house at least twice. And each year, they would cycle the same route to the tall chain-link fence and turn back. Upon occasion, they would travel into Nicosia and visit the northern half of the city, where they would sit on the terrace of Café Istanbul, facing the Venetian Column, before cycling up to the Kyrenia Gate. They continued to do this, this same trip, each year in October. Regardless of anything else, Claire and her husband Otto made sure to cycle at least once to the border fence and back again to the village.

Towards the end of one September, not more than four days before Claire and Dr Canning would be returning to Ormideia, after a morning of running errands and when Daphne, if I remember correctly, had just turned thirteen, Claire unlocked her bike outside a clothing store in Jericho, in which she had bought a new dress for Elif. She put the paper bag into her basket and pushed off to ride, and as she pulled out onto the street, she failed to spot an oncoming white car, one that did not sputter but rather sped blindly into her like it were emerging from her own past.

The morning after, Daphne called me to let me know that Dr Canning had passed away. I took a night-coach from Northfield to Boston where I boarded a flight to London. It would be the first time I had returned since my mother passed, several years before, and so there was a kind of terror that was weighted by both my own self, as well as the sense of treading on the paths that I had tried to forget the bends of. Not so much did this feeling spring from having dismissed the possibility of ever returning – of which there survives a chance – but instead, I quite simply didn't foresee my return-ing happening, as I no longer foresaw much of anything. My horizon, which once seemed boundless and so distant, had all but quivered away, diminishing from many years to little more than the next hour. With this sudden and unexpected commitment came an extension, a lengthening to that hori-zon again, one in which days coagulated again, as they hadn't for so long, back into weeks, and the microscopic sense of time which I had developed in my idleness, exploded into heaving lumps of organized affairs: dinner, funeral, wake and, naturally, being with Daphne Elif Canning, for all the time she needed of me.

My plane arrived late, having been delayed for several hours on the runway in Boston. Once I landed, I took a largely empty coach from the airport into Gloucester Green. As we rattled along, I found myself oddly relieved that the motorways, the fields and hills that opened up the further you pulled away from the city, those same undulations, furrows and forests I knew so well from my childhood, were concealed under night. I was able to keep my eyes open and fall away; to be in a land that still felt foreign to me, although it wasn't. The thought of this illusion being dispelled the next morning by the eastern light caused in me a momentary panic, which was in turn softened by my exhaustion.

She had waited for me in the restaurant of the hotel. She was sat in the corner; her face only somewhat illuminated by the dim table light. Her dark and wavy hair had subtly thinned, and the taut skin of her neck had ever so slightly loosened and crumpled beneath her collar. Her dark eyes hadn't lightened at all; they hadn't paled, but instead had intensified, and were framed by her prominent temples, which appeared like shallow pits on either side of her head. Her face seemed longer; her expression dour; her hair wirier. Her white shirt poked up from beneath a wide-collared woollen jumper, and she wore long and elegant navy trousers. She asked that I stay in the same hotel as her because, as she explained to me, *I can't go home. Not yet.*

Upon first seeing her, the intervening years, those since I'd last seen her – something which neither of us could determine the length of – violently took on a different, misshapen tone in my mind; where before, the years between had seemed neat and uniform, they suddenly felt incomprehensible, faulted, collapsed. The lack of definition to them, the years in which she had grown from a young woman, struggling to play for an orchestra, to a distinguished cellist, felt to my perceptions ungraspable to me; where, contrarily, I felt my years of unfulfillment were simple for her to perceive of. We sat and spoke late into the night. She expressed to me her sadness for not being there with her father in Ormideia, although, ever since her mother had passed, she believed he preferred to go alone.

He never cycled again, she told me in her mottled international accent, *but when he was younger, in the decade or so after my mother passed, he would tell me how he would try to walk the same route they cycled together. I haven't been there in years, well over a decade now. I remember, he always took the books your mother gave to him, and occasionally he would take old ones he had never given back to her.* She chuckled at this thought. *Your mother's books were the only books he kept after he cleared away mine and my mother's. Those and his medical books. But that was it. He gave his bicycles away. We never spoke much about her. Only once, but he remained quiet, like you knew him to be. It was me who had to leave this city in the end, not him. I haven't returned in a while. I think sometimes I should've been here with him.*

When at last the waiter had come over to our table to ask us to leave, I took her arm in mine and we walked to the elevators. I left her at her door, where she explained the schedule of events I would help her with. She said once all that was done, I could go home. Without saying anything, I wondered what she thought that might mean for me. With my mother and father gone, I had found myself alone in a world I hadn't yet grown used to, and I wondered if my sense of home could in fact be found in the series of returns and recurrences that came sweepingly back to me when passing down old lanes I'd once recognized more clearly, or in the sight of the dark beam of shoreline sailing back into vision beneath me, from the comfort of a height to which the water could not rise.

I was kept awake that night by visions of the old doctor, alone and walking in that craggy town along the same narrow paths that he and his wife had walked down years before; sat on a bench in the square, listening to the conversations of women and men he no longer knew, and settled at the stone pier, watching younger men, who he had seen grow from boys, cast nets and drag in their haul. In my mind, if he did find it in him, he would drive as close as he could to the same route he and his wife once had, and then walk the remainder of the unmarked path up to the fence, where each year, he and Claire had found their cycling route bounded by the chain-link fence, the same that once she had stared through, and where he was always distracted by the sights around him, the glistening sea; he would stand where he remembered she had, or as close in his mind to that position, and look through the fence, seeking whatever part of his wife remained beyond it in the empty earth.

Two nights before the funeral, when it was still only Daphne and me, she asked that I accompany her to her father's house. I hadn't been to the Cannings' for so long and felt an odd sense of excitement at the thought of returning, although I walked with Daphne's arm tangled in mine, I could see sketched across her face a grave expression, broken only by flushes of worry. We walked in silence, down the slight incline, until at last we were both met by the sight of the house. It was dark, and so the moonlight, which reflected off the ivy that scaled up the front of the house, separated it from the dark violet night. It was a three-story house, and from the pavement, the high-pitched roof seemed to crane down over us. The red bricks seemed chalky, dusty even, gnawed away by time. Daphne asked that I unlock the door and allow her in alone for a moment before following, and so I watched as she slowly, hesitantly wandered inside and quickly was lost to the darkness of the corridor, before a light switched on.

As a child, whenever I was inside the Cannings' home, I always imagined it to be a house built on unfused and imbalanced blocks. And in storms, or when rain lashed at it, I always felt that the house – perhaps owing to its narrowness – was swaying in the wind. I stood outside on the pavement, looking off further down the road while Daphne inspected the interior. After several minutes, she emerged at the great red wooden door, and gestured for me to follow her in.

There was a cutting chill in the house. Each room, despite now being illuminated by the warmth of the lights, still seemed edged with a certain darkness. Daphne tinkered with the fireplace in the front room. I remained in the corridor, taken by the fact that the house had largely been kept exactly as it was when I had last seen it, when as a mere boy, after dinner, my mother and Dr Canning would still be sat around the table, as I with Daphne stormed loudly up and down the stairs. The floors, as I remembered them, were made up of withering planks of wood, which were covered with layers of various Turkish-styled carpets. As I looked down the corridor, which led into the kitchen and dining room, I felt that if I wanted to, I could envision Otto and my mother to be sat there, over half-eaten plates of food, talking in cautious tones, about things Daphne and I neither knew nor cared about. Only then, seeing that same old shadowed corridor after so long, did I suddenly become filled with an urge to ask my mother what it was they had spoken about. And although I don't remember, I think perhaps I did vocalize this thought, because Daphne emerged from the other room and asked, *What did you say?*

I told her it was nothing and for a moment, a brief moment, we looked deeply into each other's eyes. She seemed to see me, to truly perceive of me, and I her for the first time since that night in the pub garden when she and I were young and she told me about her mother and her father, after I had asked her a question that my mother had earlier that day asked me about her father. That was when I believed we had last seen each other, although she said it was more recently than that, but I wonder, looking back on that moment in her childhood home, if she had merely envisioned me, and believed I was there, or if she had dreamt it and it became true, or if she had been kept awake by visions of us, or if our phone calls over the years had amalgamated in her mind into a physical meeting. In truth, it didn't matter to me or to her. In that moment, I saw her as a little girl, who when she talked had to shake her head to still her thoughts, and who knew the stories so well of her mother and of her father. The same such stories that, over the years, have proliferated in me, and latched onto me; ones, as happens sometimes, that I cannot tear myself from; I cannot escape, no, they remain, even now, tangled in me and essentially so, as if they inexplicably sustain the very mechanism that causes each foot, each day to move in front of the other, and each breath to pull in only, at last, to release again.

I followed her from the corridor into the front room. She kindled a fire, which had begun roaring in the wrought-iron fireplace, in that way, at the beginning of a fire, where the logs appear untouched but are entirely engulfed in flames, seemingly enduring, even if only momentarily. I noticed atop the same worn-in sofa, a slim, A5-sized brown book was laid carefully. My old friend gestured for me to open it, which I did, and inside were a number of photographs of Claire and Dr Canning when younger. I flipped through the pages, and in them found ones of me as a child, stood beside my mother, or sat at a table with Dr Canning and Daphne. Looking back at my younger self, as well as the young and smiling face of my mother, I was overcome with a feeling of all those sunken images, those drowned moments resurfacing, gasping for a breath, before again they'd descend, out of sight, and out of mind.

We remained there in the front, talking before the fire. Daphne gave me a picture of my mother and me to keep. Around 11 p.m., we decided to put out the fire and return to our hotel. With her arm in mine, we made our way up the incline, and back towards the centre of the city. We walked in silence, both of our minds coloured by the thought of the time that without our noticing had unquestionably folded into two distinct and faraway points – our childhoods and now – the time between, those same such intervening years, seemed not to vanish in us, but instead, to fall away, to sink out of sight, even if only for that moment.

Several days after the funeral, Daphne returned to Germany. I am not sure what stirred me to do so, but I remained for some time afterwards alone in Oxford. I checked into a smaller, cheaper room at the Balkan Lodge, not a few streets from where my mother had lived. In the evenings, I walked outside her home and found myself looking up into the window of the room which had once been my own and remembered her quietly rising and turning off the lamp near my bed, after reading from a book, then her words, which always came through the darkness – *Good night*, just as I had slipped into the world of dream – and sounding both as light and as rich as they do now.

On my final day at the Balkan Lodge, a slim package arrived for me. The address was written in Daphne's usual hurried hand, with a return address in some place called Weststadt. As I sat on the edge of my bed, I carefully pulled away the tape and shook out the contents onto my lap, where landed a tattered, thin pale-yellow book with dirtied edges bound in cloth and a small note:

This came back with what they found on him on the beach.
Love, D.

There was no title on the front, nor on the spine, but I instantly recognized the book as being one of my mother's. It was the same book that she would read that old poem to me as a boy. But the book was now so old, the pages coarse and cracked; some of their corners had begun to fleck away over time. Gently, I held it and turned it over and over in my hand, imagining the places my mother's hands had once been. I opened it to its title page and read the name of that same old ballad and the name of the author, C.3.3. I turned to the start of the ballad, but almost as soon I did the entire page disintegrated into no more than a few shards of paper in my hand, as though mere touch alone could do so. I turned softly onto another page and the same happened again, a little pile of yellow pieces of paper fluttered down onto the bare floor between my feet. For a moment, not more than a second, I stopped and caught the words *does not die* as they spun onto the hard stillness of the floor. Gentler again, I turned another page, and again, even this time with the slightest touch, the page broke apart into a thousand irretrievable markings of ink and white space. Seeing my gentleness was no help, I became possessed by a sudden and destructive urge. I flicked through the pages, quicker and with more vehemence, trying to catch what I could of those old crumbling words, those same few that have always returned to me, until at last, I reached the end of the book and saw there were no pages left between the tattered pale-yellow covers anymore. Only was there a scattering of broken pieces left between my feet; some were stuck to the leg of my trousers, some still on my lap. As I looked down at the seemingly weightless mound of shattered words, my body was consumed by an unshakeable stillness. I held my breath. My eyes remained tethered to the meaningless mess of paper and ink that to me looked like a small ridge of sand in a desert, ancient and insubstantial. In that moment, I dared not move nor stir. I dared not so much as breathe nor quiver. I felt myself diminish, as if, even momentarily, I had disappeared along with the words. I was struck with fear, a fear that all the words and all the images that silently flickered behind my eyes, and so me too, could easily blow away, yes, quite easily, and in any direction, perhaps to nowhere at all, aided by nothing more than the same soughing wind that had brought them all back to me over and over and over again.

Acknowledgements

Thank as ever to my agent, Tracy Bohan, at The Wylie Agency for your belief in me and this work. I couldn't be more grateful to have found you along the way. To Tucker Smith for our fortuitous meeting and all your efforts in extending the reach of this book, and to Ben Oldfield – your concision, clear eyes and focus have elevated these pages far beyond what I thought was possible for them.

To my editor Jason Arthur and the whole team at Granta for all their support and enthusiasm in putting this book together. To Eric Obenauf and the team at Two Dollar Radio. A special thanks to Ali Smith whose generosity and attention taught me so much when assembling this text.

To Tanya Larkin and the team at *Transition* magazine, in which an earlier draft of the penultimate chapter appeared.

To Petro, Jimmy and Kris and all the staff at The Cow for refuge, food and drink.

To the Stargardter-Murray-Smiths. *Mi familia*.

To my dear friends: Lachlan Douglas-Ferguson, Alex Yeates, Jack Astles-Rollins, Jimmy Madeja, Richard Thomas and Schuyler Small for your companionship and camaraderie over the years. To my siblings, Hana and Xan for your humour and strength. To Conor, for everything, always. To my Dadi and Dada.

To my beloved Bingo, for your spirit, your stories and your friendship; I know you'll tell me off for saying it but this book does not exist without you. To my Nani, always my first reader and the one who showed me the gift of this vocation; each further word I write only deepens my communion with you.

To Papa, for your brilliance and your mischief. It is you who taught me everything I needed to know about telling a story. The spirit of this text is yours. To Mum: my soul, my first love, my compass and who everything I do begins with. And to Isabella, for our despicable, sweet and boundless life. You have forever altered the way I live in this world.